I0619054

FROM A BARREN SEED GROWN

ANTHONY W. EICHENLAUB

Copyright © 2021 by Anthony W. Eichenlaub

All rights reserved. This book or any portion thereof may not be reproduced or used in any manner whatsoever without the express written permission of the publisher except for the use of brief quotations in a book review.

Print ISBN - 978-1-950542-15-4

Ebook ISBN - 978-1-950542-14-7

oakleafbooks.com

Cover Art by: Anthony W. Eichenlaub

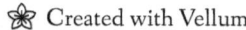 Created with Vellum

To all who have returned home only to find it changed and full of monsters.

CHAPTER ONE

BLUE SUNLIGHT DANCED across the tinted windshield of the battered spider walker, refracting rainbows of deep indigo across Ash Morgan's orange blouse. She kicked her cowboy boots up onto the dashboard and leaned back, interlacing her fingers in her wild tangle of hair, closing her eyes to enjoy the serenity of traveling over the mountainous mainland of the planet Sky.

Her heel nudged a button, and the keening high notes of jazzy brass filled the cabin.

"I meant to do that," Ash mumbled, without opening her eyes.

Hector didn't say a thing, and she could tell he wasn't upset. The big guy always tolerated her road trip mix, and, really, she'd just spent the last year and a half tending to his mortal form and keeping him alive while he orchestrated the slow waking of the entire Pyramid colony. He had saved them from eventual death, and she had kept him alive while he did it. That made them both heroes.

She cast a sideways glance at the big, wonderful guy. His beard stuck out like a bird's nest and his skin was porcelain pale for lack of sun. Stuck in the pyramid, he had lost weight, both fat and muscle, and there were a few new scars on his arms and neck, results of her many valiant attempts to help him.

"What do you think will have changed?" Ash asked as the spider trundled along over another mountaintop ridge.

Hector craned his neck to look at the other spiders traveling at their sides. Each was filled with dozens of new refugees "I don't think it'll be very different."

"Or *everything* will be different! I bet they'll have a parade when we arrive."

"That seems unlikely."

"Do you think they've built the statue of us already?"

"I read once that celebrities on Earth would become corrupted by the people's worship. It turned them into horrible, self-centered narcissists."

"Simon told me Edge's population is up to almost fifty thousand at last count, and all those new people probably think of us as heroes."

Hector's brow furrowed. "They expected to wake in paradise, and instead we woke them to a dying colony that couldn't support them, forcing the bulk of them to leave."

"And we helped them move to Edge, where there's plenty of food and everything is totally amazing." Ash watched the blue sunlight play over the windshield. "Paradise."

Hector did not look properly impressed. "I don't think Edge will be that different, but the Pyramidians might not exactly think our printed food as the hallmark of paradise."

"Everybody loves the little brown cubes, though."

"Nobody likes those."

"They have all the nutrients you need."

"True."

Ash pushed buttons until the music changed to the syncopated arrhythmic tunes of the late twenty-first century Earth. "The original Edge colonists were designed to perfectly fit their roles in society, so they had to do whatever jobs Traverse told them. The Pyramidians are going to just do whatever they want."

Hector narrowed his eyes in concentration as the spider made its way along a particularly tricky ridge. "People could always do what they wanted."

"If that were true, everyone would be a biologist."

"That's not true at all."

"Anyway, what people wanted always happened to be what Traverse wanted."

"Not everybody fit the machine's plan."

"Says the guy cloned and engineered to be a perfect boyfriend."

"I'm not—"

"You're big and strong, perfectly handsome, supremely patient, and genetically kind to a fault. All designed and produced by Traverse."

Hector drove in silence for several minutes. "I'm not genetically kind. That's not even a thing."

"You sacrificed over a year of your life so that all residents of Pyramid could be revived in a way that allowed them to start their colony back up safely."

"Anyone would do that."

"That's what a genetically kind person would say."

This brought a smile to Hector's face. "You don't really believe that, do you?"

Ash put her feet back on the floor. "I'm a genetically insensitive genius."

"Then why did you stay to help me?"

"Accolades."

Hector had no response to that, probably because it was irrefutable truth.

Life was good. Sky was good. She looked forward to nothing more than a good night's sleep in her very own house.

"Do you want to move in?" she asked impulsively. Then, when he didn't immediately answer, she added, "To my house," as if that might clarify things.

"Your house is tiny."

"My house is perfect.'

"For you. I can barely stand in there."

Ash ducked her head and hunched her shoulders. "Then just walk around like this."

"We're here," Hector said as they mounted the final rise before the colony.

The reservoir lay below them, shining in the bright-blue sunlight. It sat exactly as Ash remembered, with the shed to one side and a fusion plant a short distance away. Beyond the colony shone a vast expanse of unbroken ocean. She had missed that sight so much during her time in Pyramid.

But Edge *had* changed. It now splayed out in new directions, dominating the landscape around the reservoir and the land as far as she could see in either direction. Bulky, black buildings squatted along the upper ledge. Lithe, angular ones along the oceanside cliffs, stretching into the skies like synchronized dancers. The Commons still stood in the center of town, though a new tower jutted from atop its shining glass dome. People bustled through cobblestone streets in all manner of colorful clothing.

Colorful clothing! Ash pushed buttons on the spider's console and zoomed in on the view. People wore something other than the traditional drab gray of Edge's colonists. Could this be true? Had the larger population finally resulted in some decent attention to fashion?

But no, the fashions weren't complex or interesting. They were simply variations on the existing defaults. People wore them like uniforms. Those in green grouped with other greens. Those in blue grouped with blues.

"Look out for that barricade," she said. "You'll have to step over it."

"You mean the one that says *No Walkers Beyond This Point?*"

"Yeah, that one."

Hector set the spider down at the end of a long row of service and construction spiders. The two passenger-laden spiders parked nearby, and a small crowd gathered between them.

A man in a blue robe gestured for the group to gather. "Follow me, everyone," he said in a crisp Pyramidian accent. "From here we walk to the Commons, where you'll be assigned housing. If you can't walk that far, please let me know and I'll arrange transport."

When nobody protested, the group moved as a single mass down the path.

Ash gave them a little wave. "Good luck."

Nobody responded.

Hector said, "Sometimes heroes are intimidating."

A short distance away, a gravel path started its winding journey around the reservoir. Golden grasses surrounded clusters of short shrubs with thick, glossy leaves. Ash and Hector affixed rebreathers to their faces to filter the atmosphere's dangerous particles—still a problem, even though they had stopped the source. A flash of fur darted away as they approached, reminding Ash of her own guinea pig. She ran back to the spider and extracted his little carrying case from her lab equipment in the abdomen compartment. Inside, Mr. Floofers lay in stasis.

The trail changed from gravel to cobblestone to a properly paved, smooth walkway. Not far from the reservoir, small spider walkers lined the path. Some gleamed in the afternoon light, others sat caked with dust and grime. People they passed wore the colored uniforms she'd seen from afar, but nobody acknowledged the newcomers.

"Hi," she said as she passed a complete stranger.

The woman cocked her head and peered at them as they passed.

They made their way down the road that meandered through the rocky mountain pass. Black structures jutted from granite ridges like barnacles from a ship's hull. As Ash and Hector wandered past, they attracted stares from strange faces. Not hostile stares but looks of curiosity and wary apprehension followed them everywhere.

"I don't think I've ever *not* recognized everyone in Edge," Ash grumbled.

"They say you can't step into the same river twice," said Hector.

"This isn't a river, and it doesn't feel like home. Everything's different." Ash gestured at the city below as they rounded the corner. In the sunset, buildings took a hazy cast, their colors drained nearly to gray. "Wait a second."

"What?"

"Am I a small-town girl moving to the big city?"

Hector blinked slowly.

"Here for adventure in the city that never sleeps." Ash spun, her loose coat flaring out.

Hector chuckled. "Innocent girl on her grand adventure."

"Do you think they'll have nightclubs and gambling halls?"

"I'm sure you'll find plenty of dens of ill repute."

"Underground kickboxing rings?" Ash did a couple kicks at the air. A pair of strangers flinched, even though she wasn't even close to kicking them. "I've been practicing, you know."

Hector said, "I was there, remember?"

"Oh, were you?"

He stuck his arms out at his sides, mimicking the pose he'd had on the big machine. "I was this guy."

Ash scratched her chin. "Oh yeah, I remember you. I didn't think you were paying attention."

He shrugged. "You practiced mostly naked. How could I *not* pay attention?"

She rushed to him, jumped up on a rock, and planted a kiss on his lips. They stayed there, lost in each other for all of time, or until the sun finally set, whichever came first. When she finally pulled away, someone behind her cleared their throat.

"Hey, Simon," Hector said.

Simon wore a dark-blue suit of a smooth velvety material. The tails of his coat hung almost to his knees, and he'd added a touch of flare along the collar that complemented the silky style of his neck-length hair. He looked so absolutely huggable that Ash jumped down and wrapped him right up. After a couple excruciating seconds, he hugged her back.

"Good to see you," he said as he pulled away. He wasn't wearing a rebreather, which struck Ash as very odd.

She took her own off and sniffed the air. "It smells funny. Did Edge always smell like burnt oranges?"

"Fancy tech," Simon said. "I'll explain later, but you don't need rebreathers in town anymore."

"Oh Simon, I have *so* much to tell you. Should we go get drinks? Can we get drinks? Are there places of ill repute where we can get a drink? Something strong. I've been away over a *year*, Simon, and I haven't had hardly anyone to talk to except Hector in all this time, and there so much that I've been working on and so much that I've been doing, and I haven't really had anyone to tell about it and I want to hear all about what's been going on in Edge and Hector... Hector—"

"Doesn't talk much," completed Hector.

"He doesn't!" Ash said. She closed her mouth when Simon gestured for her to stop. Then she opened it again. "Home," she said. "My house first. Then drinks."

But Simon's smile turned sad.

"What?" Ash asked.

Simon glanced in the direction of the setting sun. Above, three moons sat dully in the hazy sky. "You can't go to your house right now."

Ash crossed her arms and took a step back. "Why not?"

Simon said, "That neighborhood is dangerous. From the old jailhouse all the way up to the start of the reservoir path."

A streetlight Ash hadn't even noticed flickered to life as shadows threatened to swallow the city. In the pool of its glow, Ash studied Simon's features. He had to be joking with her, but he had never been very good at that sort of thing.

"Good," she said. 'I've grown accustomed to living dangerously." She started strolling down the path toward her home.

"Ash, wait," Simon called, trying to catch up. Hector followed close behind. "I'm serious. You can't go there tonight."

"Look," Ash said, gesturing at the light above them as it, too, flickered to life. "It doesn't matter that it's at night because there are lights." She patted the baton that she carried at her hip. "And I've printed a new baton. What could possibly be dangerous on the way to my house?"

The whites of Simon's eyes shone against the bright streetlight. "I didn't talk about it in the messages I sent because I didn't want you to worry."

"Worry about what?"

"It's not like they're bad people, but things are tense, and—"

"Hector just spent the last year rescuing the Pyramidians from their eternal hibernation. Why would they bother me?"

Simon frowned. "True, but—"

"But Hector deserves some respect." Ash poked Simon's chest. "And he's going to get it, so we're going to my house and we're going to sleep."

Hector raised his hand sheepishly. "Actually, I just want to go to my house."

Ash turned on her heel and walked away.

Again, Simon hurried after. "There's something else. It's not *safe*."

She waved him off.

"I'm serious. You've always lived at the edge of the colony. Well, the colony didn't really grow that direction, so you're still on the edge of the wilderness."

"Wilderness?" Ash spun on him. "This is a dead planet. There's nothing out there to be wild."

His voice went quite serious. "We don't think it's coming from outside the colony."

"Maybe you should listen to him," Hector said. "You can come with me."

But all Ash wanted was her cozy little home. She'd been dreaming of it for a year, hoping that she'd be able to return and simply exist in a space that was all her own.

"Things are different here," she said, "but this is stupid. Your weird clothes and all these strange people—that's fine. It's different. People are afraid because suddenly they don't know everyone." *She was a little afraid because she didn't know everyone.* It was unsettling. "I've been to a city where tentacled monsters sprout from the earth. I've fought for my life and won. I've fought for your life and basically come out ahead." She gestured at the city. "I've seen the world. There's never, ever going to be anything that scares me right here in Edge."

Hector and Simon exchanged a glance, and Ash sensed some hidden agreement had passed between them. This time, when she turned to leave, they didn't stop her. When she was out of sight, she ditched the path for a shortcut down a steep slope. They were going to follow, and Ash needed some time alone. For the first time in a year, she needed distance.

She started along the long perimeter path as the last dregs of the setting sun cast green shadows over the strange city that had once been home.

CHAPTER TWO

STREETLIGHTS SPUTTERED LIKE DYING CANDLES, throwing buildings into gray-black shadows against an all-encompassing dusk. Shimmering moons shone with icy intensity, the three smallest ones—two silver, one a dusky red—gazing upon Ash like judging eyes. A smoky haze hung among the boulders and buildings, a blanket of incense and heavy musk.

And Ash was alone.

She'd been alone plenty during her year away. Once the systems were stable, Hector hadn't needed constant attention. She'd wandered the pyramid and even explored the nearby ruins. Through the year, more and more of the Pyramid settlement had been restored, but there were always places to go to sit alone to grasp at the hurricane of ideas crashing through her head. That was nothing like this.

Her footsteps fell with muffled echoes on the dusty path, drown out only by the thunderous pounding of her heart in her ears. If anything dangerous lurked out there—a monster, a person, or whatever—it would certainly sense the irrational fear oozing from her pores. Fear itself might kill her before she found the safety of her little home.

The path was both familiar and strange. That boulder and this ridge—they were the landmarks she remembered. Above the street, odd shapes blotted out the skyline. Inky blackness peered at her from this strange, twisted version of the Edge.

And the earth moved. Her soil-depositing blossom storms had covered the land with thin layers of dirt. Golden grasses softened corners the landscape. Cracks in the granite and the gutters on buildings were lined with tufts of feathery plants. Shrubs stood like sentinels among waving masses, exuding a sharp, musty scent.

A scuff and a scratch, somewhere in the darkest corners behind the nearest outcrop of black obsidian. Ash froze. She heard only blood rushing in her ears and the wind howling in the sky.

"I hear you following me, Simon," she said, because not speaking felt so dangerously alone. The still night air swallowed the words whole and didn't give them back.

Nobody moved in this neighborhood. In other parts of the city, far away, a dull buzz of activity bustled in the night, but only emptiness engulfed her here.

She drew a deep breath. Pyramid's media library

contained hundreds of horror films she'd never seen in the Edge archives, and she'd watched far too many of them. That surely must have caused this entirely unwarranted fear.

A growl, deep and low, echoed against the granite cliffs.

Then nothing.

She took one step, then another. Her house wasn't far, but she would never get there if she didn't move. A bath and a good night's sleep sang a siren song, drawing her forward. Hector's chamber in Pyramid had been big and dark and hollow. She longed for her cozy little home, even if it was too small for Hector to fit comfortably. It felt safe, and that was all she craved after being so long buried in the haunted hallows of the dead colony.

A few pebbles shifted on the path in front of her, and she looked up. A silhouette moved against the backdrop of the hazy moons.

"I heard you up there," Ash said, utterly failing to keep the quaver from her voice. "I'm going home, so don't bother me." There. That'll show them. She unclipped her baton anyway, and held Mr. Floofers' case up as a shield.

The streetlight above flared to full bright, blinding her. She blinked back the burning fire of white light.

And something moved. Snarled.

There was really something out there. No doubt now.

"Stay away," she said. Her voice hardened into a confidence she didn't feel. "I'm serious."

Everything outside her cone of light was swallowed by the night's encroaching darkness, except—

Except.

Golden eyes glared at her from twenty feet away. They swayed from side to side, their reflected flame dancing in a hypnotic pattern.

Her muscles ached. The safety of her house wasn't far. She could run for it.

But she wouldn't make it.

The beast took another step forward to the edge of the light and stood tall like a man. Taller than a man.

"Go away," Ash said. She had a comm unit. She could use it to call, but she'd have to let go of her baton or her makeshift shield.

Slowly, she crouched, setting Mr. Floofers' case down on the grassy path She held her baton up as if it might be a cross warding off some demon in the night.

The thing might *be* a demon in the night.

The light above flickered and at the same time, one farther ahead flared to life. A lightning-quick image of the monster flashed on her retinas.

And it was horrible. Its flesh was a yellowish, mottled color. Its shape was human, but its face was decidedly not—a twisted snarl and a million teeth. Eyes full of rage and disgust.

Ash clutched her baton in two hands until her knuckles went white.

The light flickered again. When her eyes adjusted, the thing was gone.

A voice called from far away. Shouts rang in the hazy night, swallowed in the echoes of the hills. She couldn't know where the voices came from, but she so desperately longed for the comfort of another human. It was stupid to come out here alone. Stupid to not listen to Simon. If she got out of this, she swore she'd admit her mistake to him. She pictured the look on his face when she told him. He'd be amazed.

Flicker.

Flicker.

Off.

Her eyes were ruined for the darkness, and blindness terrified her. She forgot her comm. Forgot Mr. Floofers. She clutched her baton and stumbled forward into the black, because standing still was death.

And something followed. Footsteps in the dark grated against gravel and stone.

She knew this street. She'd walked it thousands of times. Darkness couldn't stop her.

Soil twisted under her foot and she fell face-first into the weeds. She rolled onto her back, the snarling beast close. Too close.

Ash scrambled to her feet and ran. She hit the door of her house. It wouldn't open.

Muffled shouting behind her. Ash pressed her back to the door and stared wide-eyed into the black.

Boom. The wall shook beside her when something huge hit it. A peep of a scream escaped her lips.

Simon lay on the ground next to her, bleeding. Hector emerged from the dark, hands tightened into fists. Beyond, at the edge of the shadows behind him stood the creature.

It growled, "There is no mercy."

With that, it ran away into the night.

Lights flickered to life along the path. Ash could see other houses nestled among the rocks. Perfect, comfortable, safe homes, but this place was no longer safe. It stank of the monster's musk and fear suffused every stone.

Simon moaned. Lines of deep red streaked his chest. His eyes were wide with fear and his lower lip shook.

Hector knelt next to his friend.

"I'm sorry," Simon replied. "I tried..."

"You need medical attention," Ash said. "Come on."

"It's not bad," Simon whispered as she and Hector helped him up. "I'm fine."

"Why do people always say that when they're hurt?" Ash asked.

She pulled aside the shredded cloth of his shirt. The cuts weren't deep. She could slap some foam on it and it would heal fine. "We're definitely taking you in for treatment."

Simon set his jaw. "I don't need special treatment."

Ash punched him in the arm. "It's not special treatment. There could be an infection."

"I'll put foam on it when I get home."

"That's definitely not something you can do."

He stared at her, and she stared back. After a long-held breath, his shoulders slumped. "It's nice having you back, Ash. You should come with and get a place downtown."

"It's perfectly safe here!" It totally wasn't. This time she was the one to back down from the staring contest. She pretended to ignore Hector's silent amusement at their battle of wills.

Abandoning her house—Simon was right, it really wasn't safe—they made their way back to the Commons with Simon in between them. Hector probably could have carried the other man, but Ash desperately needed to help. Simon was injured and it was her fault.

"You didn't say there was going to be a monster," Ash said.

"I didn't get a chance! What did you think was out here?" Simon asked.

"I don't know. Crime statistics, I guess."

"Oh," Simon whispered. "We have that too."

"Did you see it?" Hector asked as they made their way through town.

"Yeah," said Ash, not mentioning that she saw it again every time she closed her eyes. "It was like

Skye. Older than the kid could possibly be. But the modifications. They were similar. How old is Skye now?"

"Not that old," said Simon.

"Is Skye going to grow up to be like that?" Hector took a little more of Simon's weight.

"I don't know," Ash said. Her first instinct on seeing Skye as a baby was that he was a monster. Could it be that she was right?

She had no time to think about the implications, though, because when they arrived at the Commons, they found the place packed with people. Ash nodded to a nearby bench, and they set Simon down. He gave a long sigh. From under the shadows, Ash could see the crowd gathering down the street. Many of them dressed in mixed colors and odd fashions.

"What's happening here?" Ash asked. "Why is it so busy?"

"Beats me," said Hector. "Should I take Simon through that crowd?"

Ash cast a look at her injured friend. "He's pretty tough."

Simon winced, touching his bloodied chest. "I'm fine."

"I'll take him—"

"Take him," Ash said at the same time as Hector.

After a short break, Hector got his arm under Simon's shoulder and helped him to his feet. Simon let out the long, tortured sigh of a man enduring great hardship.

"I'll come find you tomorrow," Hector said to Ash as the two hobbled down the street. "Just grab temp housing for tonight."

When they had left, a man with sunken eyes and sandy blond hair sticking out from under a polished top hat stepped from a nearby shadow. He smoothed the straight lines of his crisp black suit. "These people are here from Anvil." He spoke with a rolling growl of an accent that Ash didn't recognize. "There's been an attack."

CHAPTER THREE

"LUDOLF," said the man in the odd hat, offering a gloved hand to shake.

Ash shook and noted his fierce grip. "Ash Morgan," she said, peering at the Commons. "They upgraded this place since I saw it last."

They circled around the back where the building faced the long slope that led to the oceanside cliff. The new hospital wing formed a long, sickle-shaped arc to the east, attaching to the building under the bluish glass of the central dome. Even that dome looked different to Ash, and she thought it had maybe been upgraded to compensate for the emitter tower nestled to its northern side. Only a few refugees lingered on the downward slope of the building, and the doors there shone like gravestones in the moonlight.

Ash spotted the cantina's side entrance, hidden in the shadow of the new hospital wing. "Do you want a drink?" she asked, a little surprised that Ludolf still followed her.

Ludolf straightened his coat for the millionth time. "This place doesn't exactly look welcoming."

Ash rattled the door. Locked. "This place is always welcoming." She rattled it again.

Still locked, but this time the door opened and a familiar face poked out. "We're shut down for the night." Orson blinked when he saw Ash and a wide grin spread across the bartender's tired face. "Ash Morgan." He stepped outside and pulled Ash into a big hug.

The man's hair had gone grayer, and the loose-fitting shirt of pastel teal made his dark skin look sallow and empty.

Ash was so thrilled to see him she forgot, for one tiny instant, her manners. "That's a terrible color on you."

Orson chuckled. "It's the color I get."

"Will you let us in?"

Orson suddenly looked a decade older. "There's a whole district if you're looking for a drink this time of night."

Ash rattled the door, which had locked behind him. "Yeah, it's right here."

He sighed. "A lot has changed around here. Folks move a lot faster than they used to."

"It's not even very late!" Ash gestured at the sky as if it might win the argument for her.

Orson took her hand into both of his. The skin of

his knobby hands felt paper-thin. When had Orson aged so very much? "I'm afraid I only stay open during the day now. I'm late getting home as it is."

"All I want is a drink," Ash moaned. "And for someone to make a statue of Hector and me."

A spark of the humor Ash remembered twinkled in Orson's eyes. "Ash if they made a statue for every time you did something amazing, we'd run out of stone."

"Then you'll let us in for a drink?"

His shoulders sagged. "Stop by during the day sometime." He walked away and the dark night swallowed him whole.

"He seems pleasant enough," said Ludolf.

Ash scowled. "He's supposed to be pleasant *and* serve drinks. What time is it, anyway?"

Ludolf glanced at the sky but didn't answer.

There wouldn't be anything like sleep in her future, at least not in her own house, which was apparently surrounded by monsters. Well, one monster, anyway. Now there wasn't going to be any nectar to soften the evening. It was a nightmare.

"This is exactly how I pictured homecoming," she said.

Ludolf searched her face with a worried expression.

"I know where we can find answers," Ash said, crossing the square.

He fell in step beside her. "Are they really going to make a statue of you?"

"Absolutely yes."

The biolab doors opened for Ash without a second's hesitation, and she ushered Ludolf inside, ignoring the intrusion warnings. She breathed deep of the antiseptic undertones, and a knot inside her chest unclenched. *This* was home. *This* was where she would find peace after her long time away. "It's the smell of science," she said. She made a fist and waved it dramatically. "Of truth."

"It smells of death," muttered Ludolf.

"No death without life," Ash quipped. "And there's marginally more life here, so I think we're good."

Ludolf opened his mouth as if to say something, but the brilliance of her words must have short-circuited his brain.

The lab stood dark and empty, with many stations packed away into storage. "Or, maybe not," Ash said. Only one office glowed with soft light, so Ash led Ludolf to it. It was the science council's meeting chamber.

Or, at least, it had been when Ash left Edge. An enormous desk dominated the space, and colorful weaves shrouded the walls. Photographs of three Skyling babies stood on a broad bookshelf, their toothy grins wrinkling their lumpy noses. The people of Edge hadn't always preferred the strange children, but ever since Marta had her experimental child Skye, colonists had preferred to give their children certain biological advantages. Tougher skin, better ability to breathe the planet's air—claws for some reason. Some, like Clympia, had even produced triplets.

Olympia looked up when Ash tapped on the doorframe. Her thick, black hair was buzzed short and she wore a pair of gold-framed glasses that shone against her dark skin. A broad smile spread across her face when she saw Ash. She rushed across the room for a hug.

"You smell awful, girl," Olympia said by way of greeting. When she saw Ludolf, one of her eyebrows shot up in question. The tone of her voice dropped an octave and her smile faded. "And you are?"

"This is Ludolf," Ash said. "He's from Anvil."

Olympia waved for them to sit in front of her desk.

"What's going on here?" Ash asked, eyeing Olympia's lab equipment along one wall. "Everything's different."

Olympia sat at her desk and rotated a screen so that Ash could see it. Numbers displayed in a twisting graphical interface. "I have a lot of work to do and kids to pick up in an hour. Help me with this and I'll have time to talk."

Ash took the tablet out of its stand. She recognized the crack down one side of the screen. "Is this *mine?*"

Olympia said, "Nothing else works for detailed analysis anymore."

"I thought I *lost* this!"

"The fact that you believed that you had lost it is reason enough that you shouldn't have it," Olympia said.

Ludolf leaned forward to look at the screen. His greedy eyes took in everything until Ash turned it away from him. Something about the way he leered at her numbers made her uncomfortable.

Also, the numbers were fascinating.

"Is this the local microbiome?"

"Some of it," Olympia said.

"But there are thousands of unique factors here. How did you make all those?" Ash swiped on the screen. A quarter of the interface didn't respond properly due to the cracked glass. "This is definitely worse than when I last had it."

"Microorganism diversity skyrocketed in the last year. Both stuff falling from the sky and organisms found in random samples of the soil. Then there's that mess Pyramid made in the reservoir. Don't get me wrong, they did some good things for us, but there are these slimy things that keep crawling out."

"Frogs?" Ash asked. "Gerald must be thrilled."

"We *drink* that water." Olympia tapped a long fingernail on her desk. "It's been a long year, Ash."

But Ash wasn't listening. They'd taken samples from all over town, digging through the newly created soil. Certain spots contained extremely varied organics—levels similar to what she'd read about in the soils of Earth. Still mostly focused on the screen, she said, "Oh, a monster attacked Simon."

Olympia stood.

Ash glanced up. "He'll be fine. Hector took him in for treatment. Simon didn't want to go, but we made him, even though there were all those people from Anvil."

"Good," Olympia snapped. Ash thought there was more bitterness in the response than necessary. "People from Anvil?"

"Some kind of attack. I thought there would be more scientists here in the lab," said Ash.

Ludolf cleared his throat. "I only just arrived, but they say there have been rumors of monsters outside Anvil for a long time."

Olympia sat back down, but she hovered on the edge of her seat. "Traverse hasn't made any recordings of the events. Reports of it started about six months ago. There were rumors of something outside of town stealing food."

"Oh, a cyanobacteria," Ash said poking at the screen. "Well, good luck finding nitrogen in *our* atmosphere."

"We never caught it on video. Even when people swore that they'd seen it within the video's recording arc, we found nothing." Olympia nodded at the screen in Ash's hands. "Not even on your unfiltered screen."

Ash peered at the tablet. "This screen doesn't lie."

Ludolf's brow furrowed. He clearly wasn't

following the conversation, and Ash felt a little bad for him.

She turned the screen to him so he could see the data. "Uncorrupted data. It's really nice." She hid the screen again when he looked at her numbers a little too greedily. "The video Traverse gives you is always edited. The older it is, the more edited. Data, even hard numbers, tend to get corrupted and strange when Traverse is working hard on changing a story. It's one of the quirky things we love about our robot overlord."

"You—like that?" Ludolf furrowed his brow.

"No. But come on, Ludolf. You can't just *say* that you're terrified of your all-knowing all-seeing AI overlord."

"I see." Ash was sure he didn't.

"I thought they made this part of the standard education in Anvil." To Olympia, Ash said, "You could have told us we were sending too many people from Pyramid. Hector would have slowed the waking process."

"Construction and food production kept up, so we saw no reason to stop you. If we had, you'd still be there taking people out of stasis." Olympia pinched the bridge of her nose. "Things have gotten messy, but we're doing fine."

"Except for occasional monster attacks," Ash said.

"One of those people you woke must have been a little crazy."

"Most of them, as far as I could tell." Ash lowered the tablet. "There was this guy—"

Olympia cut her off with a sharp gesture. "People moved inward from the outskirts of town. We build up instead of out now, and with access to Pyramid's tech it's not difficult. It means people don't have room to grow their own plants or raise their own animals, but that's fine for now."

"People raise animals?"

"The guinea pig population has skyrocketed."

Ash remembered Mr. Floofers. When she noticed Ludolf and Olympia staring at her, she shrank into herself. "I dropped Mr. Floofers when the monster attacked."

Olympia leaned forward and peered at Ash over interlaced fingers. "Tell me more about this attack."

"I assume it'll sound a lot like every other description you've heard."

"This is the first time someone I know personally has experienced an attack. Everyone else has been from Pyramid or Anvil, and descriptions have been —varied."

It had all happened so fast, but she still had that flash of an image burned into the back of her eyes. "It was a Skyling, Olympia. Ridged nose flaps, yellow eyes. Teeth and claws."

Olympia frowned in concentration. "You think was one of the Skyling kids? Was it Skye?"

Ash peered at the screen. "If the cyanobacteria fixes nitrogen, then what are these other bacteria?"

"Focus."

"Oh, um, no of course not. Skye's just a little kid."

"He's bigger now than when you last saw him," said Olympia. "And so are my three. They grow fast." Olympia had three Skyling children. Skye had been the first, but Olympia's three had followed shortly after.

"Like predators?" Ash asked.

"You should go visit Skye," Olympia said.

Ash let herself be distracted by the tablet again, falling into the beautiful arrays of numbers.

Ludolf stared at the pictures of Olympia's three Skyling children. "Your children..."

"They're a handful," Olympia said, her tone icy "Climbers."

"Are there more like this?" Ludolf asked, tugging at the collar of his suit.

"More all the time," Olympia said. "Last I heard there were a couple mothers due soon, which should bring the total to an even hundred."

"There are a hundred Skylings?" Ash asked.

"You'd have to ask the hospital if the new ones have arrived yet." Olympia glanced at her screen. "But, it's almost time for me to pick mine up from Allan," she said, shutting down her systems. "You two are welcome to come with if you like."

Ludolf stammered and took a step back.

"We'd love to." Ash put an arm around his shoulder. She whispered, "Ludolf, you didn't tell me you were new to the planet."

He stammered, "Well, I—"

"It's probably best if you get used to how things are here. Let's meet Olympia's kids, then we'll go see if the line for housing is any shorter."

Olympia threw a stylish pea coat over her shoulders and gathered a pack with her things. When she went into the other room to shut down the equipment, Ash disconnected the tablet and stowed it in one of her many pockets.

Ludolf blinked. "Are you supposed to—"

Ash shushed him. "Let's go."

Olympia led them out of the lab into the streets, where the town still felt alive in the flickering streetlights. The air was heavy with the smell of fried bread, seared guinea pig, and roasted vegetables. The whole medley made Ash slightly nauseous, and every twenty steps someone she knew from Edge greeted her with far too much enthusiasm.

"They really eat guinea pigs?" Ash asked, eyeing a stand where a man sold skewered meat.

"The Pyramidians dislike printed food," said Olympia. She glanced at Ludolf. "Anvilites will eat literally anything."

Ash glanced at Ludolf, but the man didn't respond to the comment

She tried not to imagine processing Mr. Floofers into one of the meat skewers. The fact that the food smelled so amazing made everything so much worse.

Oddly, there in the center of town, among the

bustling crowds, she felt less safe than she had being stalked by the monster near her home. She wondered if she could ever feel safe again, between the pressures of her changed life and the new dangers encroaching. She *almost* longed for her chamber in Pyramid where she and Hector wiled away days watching media and joking about all the travel they would one day do.

"Allan," Olympia said as she entered the nursery, "you remember Ash, right?"

"Of course," said a burly man with a beard like a black wire brush.

Ash recognized him from when she used to pick up Skye for their days together. A wave of apprehension washed over her. "Is Skye here?"

"Home already." He ushered them into the cozy space. "Esther, Octavia, Mav, your mother's here."

Three Skyling children ran out of the playroom to mob their mother. All three were the modified humans suited for life on Sky, but something felt different about their changes compared to the monster Ash had met in the dark streets. Maybe it was because they were juvenile, but their teeth didn't look as menacing and their claws didn't hook quite so much.

Ash opened her mouth to greet the children—she hadn't seen them since they were babies—but she caught sight of Ludolf and stopped.

His face was a mask of barely controlled fear.

Ash took his arm. "What's wrong?"

He blinked. "Surprised is all. I saw the pictures, but..."

"They're not that bad. Don't let them bite you."

"I'll wait outside," Ludolf said, backing away. He retreated into the street, twisting his hat in his hands.

"What's your friend's problem?" Olympia whispered.

"I just met him." Ash smiled at the kids. "Wow, you've all grown so big!"

"They do that." Olympia peeled the children from their hug one by one. "Kids, this is Auntie Ash. She's been away awhile, but she was around when you were born."

All three mumbled something, then one—Esther, Ash thought—stepped forward. "Hi, Auntie."

"Hi, Esther," said Ash. She knelt and spread her arms. The girl piled into her for a hug. After a brief hesitation, the other two children did the same. "I'm happy to meet you again."

Exhaustion finally caught up with Ash. She separated from the children and said, "I better go find a place to live before I crash."

"I'm sure there's plenty of temp housing," Olympia said. "Will you be staying with Hector?"

"He's with Simon. We'll meet up tomorrow."

Olympia sighed. "I'd better go pick up my fearless warrior, too, huh?"

"It was a pretty shallow scratch," said Ash.

"But he's *such* a whiner."

CHAPTER FOUR

"TRAVERSE," Ash said, speaking to the colony's AI for the first time in ages, "Tell me about the monster."

The *T* logo on her tablet spun quietly for several seconds. The temporary quarters designed for newcomers weren't openly hostile to their residents, but they weren't exactly what Ash considered friendly. She had a bed, a small food printer, a media screen on one wall, and a distinct lack of bathtub. It had been a comfortable enough place to sleep overnight, and with the desert dust scrubbed from her skin under the weak shower, she almost felt normal. The clothing printer embedded in one wall had almost a dozen pre-configured styles, all in the vast variety of colors ranging from dark blue to almost black.

It took her an hour to hack past the restrictions, and as her new outfit printed, she did her best to question Traverse.

Finally, the AI responded, "The monster—referred to more often as the creature, the fiend, the spectre, the dæmon, and the devil—was the invention of Mary Shelley in the first of an era of science fiction horror."

Ash sighed. "Not Frankenstein."

"Bram Stoker's Dracula—"

"No."

"The mummy—"

"Quiet!" The logo spun quietly for a long time. When Ash's irritation faded, she said, "Give me video around my house last night just after sunset."

The video appeared immediately. She saw herself creeping through the dark streets, looking like a vagrant. Simon and Hector trailed a short distance back in that patronizing way overprotective friends tended to do. If she had known they were following, she probably would have told them to scram. She could handle herself, after all.

Except, of course, when she couldn't.

The camera blurred. A flash of light blew the exposure limiters and several frantic seconds passed with only a jaggy motion blur on an almost-white screen.

There was no image of a monster, just as Olympia had warned. Ash brought up the text log on her tablet. "Is this video modified?"

No warnings flowed past the screen when Traverse answered, "No." Not a lie, then. Interesting.

If the video wasn't modified, then the flashing lights really had disrupted the camera's function.

But the flash had happened immediately *before* the attack.

"Traverse, why aren't the streetlights working properly?"

The logo spun. In the lower corner of the screen, a small clock appeared.

"Oh." Time to go. Ash grabbed her new clothes from the printer—a leather coat with reinforced lining, a button-down blouse, and a pair of heavily reinforced pants, which turned out to be a terrible idea. When the pants hung too heavily on her hips, she swapped them for a sleek pair of bell-bottoms in the standard dark blue. Overall, it was a very professional style.

On her way out, she stuffed the tablet in her coat pocket. There would be time to interrogate the thing later. She clipped a new baton to her belt.

One of the biggest changes in the science council meetings, Olympia had explained the previous day, was that it no longer met in the mostly abandoned biolab. Nor did it meet in the moderately abandoned chemlab, botanylab, or physicslab. Instead of showing a strong bias for the obviously superior science of biology, the council met in the most unscientific building in the colony: the Archives.

Moira Heartell ushered Ash into squat the building with a dark scowl. The click of the tiny, white-haired woman's shoes echoed against the high vaulted ceiling. The Archives, unlike every other building in the colony, extended downward into solid stone. The levels of protection for the colony's hidden secrets were absolutely ridiculous. It almost made Ash want to organize an exciting heist, but she stopped herself from mentioning this to Moira.

"Elevator," said Moira.

"Are you my escort?" Ash gave a super polite bow, which was not sarcastic in the least.

"Simon is indisposed this morning. He's out ill."

Ash blinked. "It was just a scratch."

Moira cast her a sideways glance. "Should have known you'd be involved."

"Why aren't we taking the stairs?"

"You don't get free rein to the vaults these days." The corners of Moira's mouth tightened. "There was an incident."

"Did someone steal something from the Stephen King collection?"

"The elevator will take you directly where you need to go."

At the bottom of a long, silent elevator ride, the doors opened on a meeting already in progress in a room carved from black stone. The walls bore reliefs telling the story of humankind's journey to the stars. In the center of the room, carved from the very granite itself, stood a gigantic round table, around which sat the various members of a very large council.

Leonard argued in barely contained whispers

with Olympia. His explosion of gray hair bobbed as spittle flew off his lips. Olympia absorbed the verbal assault with all the grace and class Ash had come to expect of her, then gave it back tenfold. Near them stood Jasper the botanist and Gerald the ecologist, both wearing deep-burgundy scrubs. The two men spotted her first and Jasper rested a hand lightly on Gerald's shoulder, as if to restrain him.

Juliette sat as far from Jasper as possible, possibly an indication that the two were not together anymore. Another reminder of how much Edge had changed. Ash wondered what the food worker was doing in the science council.

"Food science," Juliette said when Ash pushed her way over through the crowd. "It's a real science."

"Real sciences don't need to go around claiming to be real science," Ash said, keeping her tone light. She appreciated seeing a friendly face. Juliette had been on the trip to Pyramid. She'd been one of the first to understand Ash and Hector's sacrifice and what it meant for Edge and the other colonies. "Who are these people? Does Victor have a line in to communicate?"

"Victor isn't very popular these days." Juliette pointed to each of the others at the table, "Naomi from Anvil, a materials engineer. Bastion, Polard, and Poole are all neuroscientists of some sort from Pyramid. I have trouble telling them apart. And over there is Tobin."

Ash eyed the man Juliette pointed to last. He was

a young man whose slender figure was accentuated by his tight white suit. "What does he do?"

"Everything, if you hear him say it." Juliette smiled. "You should get along great."

The elevator door slid open, and the chatter in the room stopped. Palak stepped out, followed by her giant brother Harish. Both wore stiff, brown tunics, with matching leggings and armbands. A long tube of a weapon—the only energy weapon Ash had ever seen on Sky—was strapped to Palak's back, draped in her long, brown hair. It showed wear from its years of use, but she imagined Palak kept it in good working condition.

The mole on Harish's upper lip danced when he almost smiled at the sight of Ash. A pang of guilt impaled Ash's heart. The man still towered over his sister, the bulk of his muscle almost as intimidating as the intensity of her gaze. Ash had once nearly gotten him killed, but he seemed happy to see her.

"Councilors," said Olympia, "I've asked the Anvil ambassador Palak to come describe to us the dilemma from last night." She gestured to Palak, who stepped forward.

"Thank you, scientists of Edge. I hope I will not take too much of your valuable time." Her words were stilted, and Ash caught the hint of a nervous stutter.

Ash whispered to Juliette, "Why does this feel so formal?"

Juliette shushed her.

"Last night," Palak said, "Anvil suffered an attack. There had been reports for months of creatures lingering in our outskirts, but nothing prepared us for what happened."

Tobin scoffed and crossed his arms. He whispered something to the frowning man—Poole—next to him.

Palak continued, "Their howls echoed in the hills before the attack, which happened as the day's geologists and engineers spread out across the terrain to perform a test."

"Do you have evidence of this?" asked Tobin.

"I have reports of a dozen dead colonists, Mr. Frank," Palak spat, dropping the formal tone. "Are they not evidence enough?"

"Not unless I can see their wounds. Not unless I can watch video of the attack. This is all tragic, but more rumors bring very little of practical use to this council or this colony."

Palak clenched a fist.

Tobin gestured permission for her to continue.

"To answer your question further," Palak said, "no recording was captured of the creatures, either on video or audio. It was as if they were edited from Traverse's video logs. We also found no evidence of such editing, according to our best experts."

Ash whispered, "I bet I could find evidence."

Juliette scowled at her. She put a finger to her lips.

"I used to be an investigator, you know," Ash whispered. "I solved a murder."

"Will you—"

Olympia cleared her throat and glared at Juliette.

"Sorry," said the food scientist.

Palak continued, "The attack came as the seventh moon cleared the horizon in the early hours before morning. The creatures approached from the north, near the schoolhouse where they cut down several people before rampaging through town. They struck like lightning, according to those who saw it."

"But you saw nothing?" Tobin interrupted.

"Most fled for their homes, which, like yours are sturdy and generally safe. Those who were in the field could not flee toward town. They instead fled this direction and have been graciously housed by Edge."

"Were people attacked along the way?" Ash asked, unable to keep her curiosity at bay.

"Harish and I interviewed many who fled. They were hounded by the creatures most of the day, but they were not attacked."

"But did you see the attackers? Did anyone?" asked Tobin. "We don't even know if this is an animal or a machine at this point. How can we defend against it?"

"It wasn't a machine," Ash whispered, the monster's horrible face flashing before her eyes.

Palak glanced at Harish, but the big man gave a single shake of his head. "The dead had claw and bite marks. Many victims were torn to shreds." He drew a deep breath. "Anvil does not have the resources of a large colony like Edge. We have very few people able to fight at all, and our only makeshift weapons are those we have forged from the mountain's ore."

Olympia said, "Edge doesn't have weapons."

"But you could. And you have people who could be defenders."

Tobin said, "Edge has no resources for a proper defense. Especially not if we know so little about the attacker."

"We know they eat people," Palak hissed. "Is that enough?"

A murmur rippled through the crowd.

Tobin addressed the council. "This bears more investigation. I propose we send walker drones out to seek these *monsters* and if we find them, then we can study their behavior."

"You need to send Anvil help so they can build a better defense," said Palak through her teeth. "And weapons."

"We've been over this before," said Tobin. "Engineering will not make weapons."

"Override them," Palak said.

Olympia held out a hand and the room went quiet. "Traverse forbids us access to weapon designs."

Palak drew her energy weapon and held it up for everyone to see. "Then replicate this, and design new weapons. Use all your ingenuity to make something *useful* for a change."

"It's not so simple," said Olympia.

"People have died," snapped Palak. "And you do nothing."

Tobin leaned back in his chair, looking smug about having proven his point. "We can send the drones."

Palak growled, "You need to send an army."

"I've seen one," said Ash, but her words were drowned in the chatter of the scientists.

"We don't have an army," said Olympia. When the voices rose, she repeated louder, "We don't have an army. We can't."

"This is a scientific community," Tobin purred. "That's been explained plenty of times. We send research drones or we send nothing."

Palak shouted, "That's not enough! Anvil sent walker drones and found nothing."

"I've seen one of the monsters," Ash repeated. "Right here in Edge."

The scientists all looked to her, and Ash felt very small.

She stood to address the group. "This is not how I expected to spend my first day back in Edge. Edge isn't what I left. This place has changed, and I don't know if you've all figured out how much." She addressed Tobin directly, ignoring the smug expression on his punchable face. "I was attacked last night on my way home. The creature stood like a man but had claws and teeth." She stopped herself before making the comparison to the Skylings. The new branch of humanity had enough trouble integrating, as evidenced by Ludolf's reaction the previous night. "It wasn't a machine."

"And who are you?" asked Tobin.

"It stood about a head taller than me. Well-muscled and with numerous facial modifications which possibly accounted for its ability to survive in the wastes. The way it breathed—I think it had an extra set of filters for breathing."

Tobin stood and placed his fists, knuckle down, on the stone table. "How could you possibly know that?"

"We were quite close," Ash said.

He looked her up and down. "You said you were attacked."

Olympia cleared her throat to get their attention. "What Tobin means, Ash, is that it seems implausible that you'd get away without a scratch when so many others have died."

"I've been practicing kickboxing." When Tobin didn't respond, she continued, "Hector and Simon were there. They can verify my account."

"Simon can't," Olympia said. "He's unconscious."

"Well, he's the reason I got away, so, if you want proof, look at his wounds," Ash said. "Simon's a hero."

Olympia raised an eyebrow impossibly high. "Is this the same skinny person I'm married to?"

"Did the lights flash before the Anvil attack?" Ash asked Palak.

All at once, the scientists all started talking.

"Quiet!" Olympia said, and the group complied. "We've heard enough to make our decision. Palak, Harish, you may leave, unless there is something else you feel we should know." There was not, so the brother and sister exited via the elevator. "We will take a short recess, and then vote on whether or not we need to execute our prepared plan."

"What plan?" Ash whispered to Juliette.

"You don't need to whisper now." She turned to discuss something with the scientist on the other side.

The others broke into smaller groups, chattering among themselves, leaving Ash awkward and alone. Who could have imagined she would feel out of place among her people? She made her way toward Olympia, greeting Jasper and Gerald along the way. The two men clung closely to each other, and Jasper smiled at her approach.

"Together now?" Ash asked.

Jasper gripped Gerald's hand tighter. "On our good days," he said.

Gerald wouldn't meet her gaze, but that was normal for him.

Ash continued around the perimeter until she found Olympia, who sat with open palms pressed to her eyes.

"It's some kind of infection," Olympia said, sensing her approach. "You weren't wrong about Simon's injury being shallow."

"I wasn't worried about being wrong."

"You know you were, Ash." Olympia looked up at her. "Being wrong is the thing you hate most in the entire world."

"I'm not a huge fan of getting attacked by monsters."

Olympia whispered, "Thank you for not comparing it to my children."

"Those kids don't need any more trouble." She thought of Skye and wondered if she could visit him after the meeting. Or, maybe later that day. "I bet they make enough trouble on their own."

"They don't need to." When Ash didn't respond, she continued, "There was some trouble a while back. Some Pyramidians gave us a hard time. Simon's still pretty worked up about it."

"Pyramidians don't like your kids?"

"More like some of them aren't nice people, and we're still figuring out what to do about it."

Ash slid into the chair next to Olympia. She whispered, "What's the deal with this Tobin guy?"

"Hotshot from Pyramid. He's smart. Not great at picking up social cues. Kind of a jerk know-it-all most of the time." Olympia flashed a mischievous grin. "Reminds me of someone I know."

"Who?"

Olympia stared at Ash.

"Well, if you're not going to tell me, I'd like to go check on Simon." Ash stood to leave. "Infections are my specialty."

"You took the tablet," Olympia whispered.

"Maybe that other guy stole it."

"Ludolf."

Ash took a step toward the elevator. "I need to check on Simon."

"And I need that tablet back." For a brief fraction of a second, Olympia appeared as frazzled and exhausted as Ash knew anyone else would have been in a similar situation. Then, all at once, it disappeared, and Olympia composed herself like an ebony statue standing against a storm. "We'll talk later."

The elevator doors had almost closed when Tobin stuck out a fist to stop them. "You've really messed things up, you know," he said. His breath smelled like sour apples.

"Sometimes a scientist needs to adapt a hypothesis when new information comes in, Tobin," Ash said. She mashed the button to close the elevator door, and this time, he let it close.

CHAPTER FIVE

"But I just want to study him," Ash said.

The med tech, an older man with red hair like the kind of coarse brush that Ash might have once used to clean particularly soiled beakers in her lab, held up his hands and blocked her from the room. He wore a full-body black protective suit with shining mechanical joints, but his helmet was off. "Do you see how you're not helping? He is not an experiment."

"Simon is *always* an experiment." When the man didn't look like he would comply, she tried, "Olympia told me to come check on him and see if I could help."

"She specifically said not to let you in."

"I can help!"

"We have the best medical technology known to humankind," the tech said. "Everything that can be done to help Simon is being done. Your interference can only make things worse."

"I'm a microbiologist. Microbiology always makes things better."

"This is an allergic reaction to substances that are no longer present. We only need to subdue his immune reaction and his body will heal itself."

Ash narrowed her gaze. "No infection?"

"None."

"A protovirus?"

"Traverse's systems scan for every known infective agent and they run profiles for any foreign materials, living or otherwise. There is nothing there, and Simon is recovering."

Ash poked him in the chest. "They told me at the lab that Traverse wasn't reliable for anything anymore."

The tech shook his head. "That's for the science labs. When it comes to caring for injured patients, Traverse has always been perfectly reliable."

Behind him, down the hall, Ash heard the cries of newborn babies. "Maybe you should go take care of that."

"The new Skylings are with their mother, and don't need my help."

Ash stood on her toes so she could see over the man's shoulder. Simon lay on a bed hooked up to various beeping systems. They were taking care of him. Probably.

"Maybe he needs emotional support."

The tech crossed his arms. "He won't be getting it from you."

"I know what you're thinking, Ash," called Hector from down the hall. "Techs get really mad if you try to push your way in."

"I could punch him in the gut as I ran past," Ash said without taking her eyes off the med tech.

Hector placed an arm around her shoulder. "That won't help."

The tech glared at her. She glared back.

"I could," Ash grumbled. "And maybe give him a taste of that kickboxing I was working on in Pyramid." Even so, she followed Hector out of the hospital wing.

"You've never kicked anyone, Ash, and that guy's wearing a protective suit with a powered exoskeleton," Hector said, amusement in his voice. "It's the same suit they use over in the Fusion building. Let's let Simon heal on his own. I was with him for a while last night. All he needs is some rest."

"Fine." Ash pulled Hector down through the extended Commons to the newly decorated cantina. The reconfiguration removed all the cozy, familiar feeling of the place and replaced it with the stark, raw efficiency of white sheer walls and harsh blue light. Ash hated it. "If Simon's not infectious, then why won't they let us in? And why does that guy need a protective suit?"

Hector said, "The powered exoskeleton helps him move patients around."

"Simon's light."

"Not everyone is."

"Are they radioactive?"

"Hi, Orson," Hector said with a smile.

Orson leaned both elbows on the bar, a wide grin showing white teeth. He wore a kufi and robe as he often had, but instead of bright squares of color, his clothing was entirely a pastel teal. It made his dark skin seem off in color but complemented his eyes perfectly. "Welcome back," he said, his voice cracking with a barely concealed laughter. "We have missed the both of you very much."

Ash took one of his hands in her own. "Everything's changed, Orson."

He looked around in mock surprise. "Has it?"

"In Pyramid, I had the peace and quiet I always wished I had. I ran so many experiments, and, Orson, I made wonderful discoveries about how biology can fix this broken planet." She squeezed his hand. "But there's so much more to do and this place is so different."

Orson gave a little nod toward the wall of bottles behind him. "Sometimes it pays to slow down and take in our surroundings before rushing forward."

The wall behind Orson opened to reveal rows of colored bottles, all labeled with fancy lettering and stylized art. "I want to try one of each," she said.

Orson leaned on the bar and looked her right in the eyes. "It's good to have you back."

She stuck her thumb out at Hector. "He's paying."

"It was Tobin's idea," Hector said.

"Drinking?"

"Radiation-proof exoskeleton suits in the hospital. Very useful, from what I hear."

"Yeah, I don't like that Tobin guy," Ash grumbled into her drink.

"I thought you'd get along with him. He's a biologist."

"Yeah," she spat. "A biologist who dabbles in a dozen other sciences. He's an action science superstar if you listen to what everyone says."

"So?"

"That makes him direct competition."

Hector nodded almost exactly as if he understood.

"He's just too dragging his feet on everything," said Ash.

"Sure."

"And..." Ash couldn't think of any more complaints, which was the worst complaint of all. After a year away she came home to find her job as neighborhood eccentric was filled, leaving her feeling unfit and unwelcome. "Let's sing."

An hour later, Hector and Ash entertained the establishment with a duet of a song called "We Didn't Start the Fire," which, as far as Ash could tell, consisted mostly of shouting random words and made-up names. They were good at it, too, and their shouts harmonized perfectly with each other in a way that only veteran singers were supposed to be able to do.

When the song finished, Ash laughed. "Can you believe we've never practiced?" She looked around at the other customers. There were no other customers. "Where did everyone go?"

"They probably wanted to figure out who started the fire."

"Speaking of fire," Ash said, blinking slowly, "I'd like to try another one of those brownish-orange ones." She pointed, but the bottles across the bar wouldn't sit still.

"I thought you didn't like that one," said Hector.

"I don't, but you'll finish it for me."

He ordered two of them.

"Have you visited Skye yet?"

Ash took a sip of her drink. It was an awful, spicy thing—an overpowering avalanche of flavor dusted with cinnamon and nutmeg. She took another sip and leaned her spinning head against Hector's arm. "I can't believe how much this place has changed."

"So that's a no."

"What if he doesn't remember me?"

He swallowed his nectar and took her hand. The warmth of his touch calmed her, but it wasn't enough. "Edge is basically the same. It's just bigger."

The door opened behind them. A rush of wind and noise blew in from the open square.

"Thought I'd find you here," said Palak.

Ash jumped up to greet her friend, swayed unsteadily, and almost ran into a table that wasn't where it ought to have been. After she'd sufficiently crushed Palak in a hug, she said, "You have to try the reddish-brown one!"

"Brownish-red," said Hector.

"Brownish-red!" Ash stumbled back to her seat at the bar. Something about how her words came out didn't sound quite right, and Hector chuckled in that way he only chuckles when Ash had a few too many to drink. She flagged down Orson. "Two more reddish-browns."

"Brownish-red," Hector said.

Palak said, "Give me an ocean sunset." Her dark-brown outfit clung to her angular frame. The colony's only energy weapon—a powerful but awkward rifle— still hung on her back. Ash cast a quick glance to the case above the bar where it had once been stored and found only a replica baseball bat there.

Ash stared at Palak blankly, unable to comprehend her words. Orson fetched a flared glass from the rack, and, using a spoon to spread the liquid, poured blue nectar on the bottom, then a sequence of orange, indigo, and green.

"You can mix them?" Ash said in awe.

Palak smiled and took a sip. An expression of pure bliss washed over her face. "Orson, can you get them a round, too?"

"You don't think they've had too much?" Orson said with a smirk.

"The way things have been going around here? I think they haven't had enough."

Orson nodded and got to work.

Palak said, "Anvil's research pulled up data on dozens of varieties of nectar, and some other ways to get alcohol, and other mind-altering substances."

They sat in silence for several long seconds, which was excruciating to Ash. Finally, she said, "A lot has changed."

Hector took a sip of his ocean sunset and nodded approvingly.

"There have been problems lately. Fights." Palak stared into the depths of her glass. "Some people say it's because the Pyramidians are causing trouble."

Ash, said, "Yeah, troublemakers are the worst."

"Here's the thing," Palak said. "There's nothing outside of the colonies. At all. How would dozens of monsters even survive unless they're out there eating rocks?"

Ash took a too-big gulp of her ocean sunset. The mix of flavors hit her in waves, from sour and tart to spicy and sharp. "And if they ate rocks, why would they attack people? We're not rocks."

"I attack rocks," Hector said. His work at the quarry had always been a point of pride.

"But you don't eat people." Palak raised an eyebrow. "As far as I know."

"Sometimes I would build things from them." Hector paused to consider. "Rock, I mean."

"Not people," Ash said.

"No."

Palak shook her head. "We've tried tracking them

down. Whenever we scan for traces of them, we get nothing."

"Did the monsters really eat people?" asked Ash.

"I don't know," admitted Palak. "The reports got pretty jumbled."

Hector took a swig. "Big things. Not as big as what they're making now, though. I wouldn't know where to start."

Ash took his arm again and hugged it close. "Did you look with your own eyes?"

"We can cover more area with drones."

"Why do people keep trusting—"

Palak cut her off with a sharp wave of her hand. "The scans are better than what we would be able to find on our own."

Ash said, "Traverse is the least trustworthy machine ever made. It'll kill you if it thinks it can get a point-zero-zero-five percent better efficiency out of the colony. It's a monster of a machine, and when I looked at the video feeds of my attack, I found that it never even recorded them."

Palak blinked slowly at Ash. "We try not to talk about that."

"I *am* trying!"

"I helped make an addition to this building," Hector said, gesturing at the Commons where they drank. "It was glorious because we knew we were really making a difference. Building something solid."

"We should go to the place where I was

attacked." Ash stood carefully so Palak wouldn't think she was too drunk to walk around.

By the look of Palak's raised eyebrows, she did not succeed. Palak finished her ocean sunrise and hopped off her stool.

Hector paid their tab. "Thanks, Orson."

"You have always been my most entertaining customers," said the old man. He placed both hands on one of Hector's meaty fists. "Building things really made you happy, didn't it?"

Hector nodded.

"Then you should keep doing it."

"There's nothing to build. It's all automated." His voice dropped, and Ash heard emotion tightening it. "It always could have been automated."

"If you weren't needed, then maybe it's important to think about why you were *wanted*. We value what we build for ourselves, Hector."

"But does anyone else value it?"

Orson's eyes sparkled when he smiled. "Only one way to find out."

CHAPTER SIX

THE BLUE SUN shone *especially* bright that afternoon. Ash noticed because it burned right through
her skull and set a throbbing headache on fire. Hector
must have felt the same because he squinted against
the searing rays.

Palak said, "Some of the new nectar varieties
cause light sensitivity."

"Ow," Ash said.

Palak shrugged.

Ash drew two canteens from one of her larger
pockets. She handed one to Hector and took a swig
from the other. The nectar burned like holy fire.

"Don't you think it'd be better to take a break?"
Palak asked.

"How else am I going to build up a resistance?"

Hector took a big swallow. "I just can't believe
these new buildings," he said, waving his flask as they
walked past a row of barnacle housing attached to the

side of a cliff. His voice didn't slur when he spoke, but his face looked like he was concentrating very hard on every word. "Who designed this stuff?"

"Pyramidians," Palak said.

"There's no art in it," Hector grumbled.

"I think they have an elegant beauty," said Ash. "Like a fungus." It probably wasn't the right thing to say, because Hector's scowl intensified.

They walked through the streets of Edge, wandering through newer areas of town. There were tall buildings, taller than anything Edge had ever built before. Harsh blue sunlight reflected off the shining surfaces of towers that stretched high above the Commons. Jet-black structures jutted at angles, with slick steel façades presenting the flat surfaces of windows to the glimmering ocean far below. Ash took a deep swig. The city *was* beautiful. She had to admit that. Different, but beautiful.

Then, she noticed the hollowed-out eyes of colonists tracking them as they passed. Men and women huddled against the harsh wind in the nooks created by buildings that blacked out the sky. The cobblestone streets had been replaced by a gray, flat stone, which reflected the hot sunlight and felt like walking through the sterile air of a hospital.

Ash made a rude gesture at a man who wouldn't stop staring. "Why do people keep staring at me?"

"Your clothes are too colorful," Palak said.

Hector snorted. "Her clothes have always been too colorful."

"Traverse started printing monochrome clothing for people. We never really figured out the classification system, but everyone who prints their clothes gets assigned a color."

Ash didn't want to admit that she had hacked around the problem. "Maybe I had this old coat laying around."

"Sure." Palak greeted a couple of teens with a quick wave. "Some people hacked their printers at first, but after a few of them died in strange accidents it got around that the practice is bad luck."

"I only have good luck," said Ash.

Palak shot her a dirty look. "I was on that expedition to Pyramid, remember?"

Ash threw her arms up. "And that worked out great!"

Hector said, "We left Harish behind, and failed almost every objective, and ended up locking your boyfriend into a year of servitude."

"It wasn't so bad," said Hector.

"Where is Harish, anyway?" Ash asked.

"He went back to Anvil," Palak said. "He's going to help bolster their pitiful defense."

"What defense?" Ash asked.

Palak gave her a strange look. "You really have been gone awhile."

"Have not!" Ash took another swig of nectar. The flavors blended together and the medley felt strange on her tongue. She looked up at the rows and rows of more barnacle housing. "I haven't," she whispered to herself.

"There's been a faction fighting to build defensive structures in both Anvil and Edge. It's been going on for months. I *just* told you about that, remember?"

Ash didn't remember. "Yeah, I remember."

"Our report to the council finally changed enough minds that we're allowed to start construction. It's part of the plan."

"Hector wants to build things," Ash offered. "Like a wall or something."

"It would be so big," Hector said.

Palak chewed her lower lip. "That... isn't exactly what they have in mind."

"*So* big." Hector's eyes were wide.

Ash stopped in her tracks. The nectar buzz still gummed up the gears in her head, but the thoughts started to churn. "They're making weapons—"

Palak shushed her. "Remember the bit about not talking about certain things aloud?"

Ash blinked slowly. She spoke the words slowly, tasting each one in her mouth to determine whether or not she was supposed to be saying it. "Weapons. Energy and projectile weapons. For killing. Other people." She took another drink of nectar.

Palak ground her teeth. "Is this where you were attacked?" she asked, gesturing at the ground in front of them.

Ash blinked several times, then looked down the

street. "Hey, it's my house." After being inebriated most of the afternoon, it felt good having her mental capacity back up to a hundred percent. "Why are we here?" Maybe 90 percent. "Oh yeah, tracking the monster."

Palak looked at her with a flat expression.

"I have extensive tracking experience, you know," she said.

"She was the colony's second greatest detective," said Hector.

"Second?" Ash said, exasperated.

Hector shrugged.

"Was?" Ash shouted.

"Is this the place?" Palak growled.

Ash stared at the soil where Palak pointed. Then, she looked up at the streetlights. The grass in the area was trampled and the soil scuffed. "No, I don't think so," she said. "It was over there." She pointed to a place twenty feet away where the golden grasses waved gently in the wind.

Palak didn't move.

"No, you're right," said Ash after a moment. "It was probably here." She looked around. "But where is Mr. Floofers's case?" The possessive of her guinea pig's name did terrible things to her tongue.

Palak took the energy weapon off her back so that it hung loosely at her side.

Ash poked at the soil with her toe. The previous night had been dark, made darker by the ruinous flickering of streetlights. She found two tiny spatters of blood on some nearby grasses and boxed them for further evaluation. It was only when she went to take a swig from her canteen that she realized she had used it to store the evidence. She swore quietly.

Before she could say anything to Hector, he finished off the last of his drink. His apologetic look did nothing to defenc against the scathing ferocity of her scowl. Her head started to throb with the beginnings of what felt like an instant hangover.

Ash dropped to her knees and peered again at the evidence of her fight the night before. "Hector hit the monster and sent it that way. It tumbled through those grasses there, where everything's trampled. It ran south."

Palak looked to Hector, who nodded.

Ash didn't think she had the willpower to stand again, but she almost did it anyway. She probably deserved an award for the effort. She lay down on her back and pressed her thumb knuckles into her eyes.

"The new nectars all give vicious hangovers," Palak warned.

"Thanks."

Hector helped Ash up, the big man seemingly unaffected by the nectar's vicious revenge. They walked south, where evidence of the monster continued along the perimeter path. Soon, the trail looped back to another cluster of tiny houses like Ash's. Her former neighbors had all moved out, and the houses sat empty and unused.

Except for one. A shadow moved behind the

semitransparent window. Palak held out a hand to signal a stop, but Ash pushed past to knock on the door. She gave it three quick raps, waited an exceedingly long time, then knocked again.

Ash tried the door. It swung open with only the slightest pressure, and a scent like rotten fruit wafted out. The light from the sun shone directly through the door, making a painfully bright slash of light against an encroaching blackness.

Ash stepped inside. "Hello?"

Her eyes adjusted quickly to the dark when she pushed the door closed. Inky gray shadows sharpened into distinct color and shape. Whatever the nectar did to hinder her ability to see the light, definitely helped her night vision.

The main room in the tiny house was a cluttered mess. Sofa, media console, and tiny food printer all mimicked Ash's own house, but the color schemes were off and the place had a mirror image configuration. A rasp of breath sounded to her left, but Ash couldn't see its owner among the piles of excess printed debris. Atop a table in one corner sat Mr. Floofers's case. Clothes scattered on every surface clustered in the corners, and Ash had to peer closely to see if there might be something living there. She took another step closer.

Ash failed to keep the fear from her voice. "We're not looking for trouble. I just want to know if you've seen the monster that runs around this part of the settlement." She swallowed. The throbbing pain in her head faded, consumed by the darkness of the room. "We'll believe you if you've seen something. I know others have said it doesn't exist, but I know that's not true. I've seen it."

The shadows on the sofa shifted, and a pair of yellow eyes looked up at her from the darkness. A voice rumbled, "If it's a monster you seek, look no further."

And he rose to stand before her, a ruined man in bloody shreds of clothing. His eyes flashed.

"Please." He held his hands out to her, wrists extended as if in supplication. "Kill me now and be done."

CHAPTER SEVEN

"MY NAME IS KETT," said the monstrous man in a voice that rumbled like a construction spider on concrete, "and it is I who attacked you last night. I would do it again, were you foolish enough to walk these streets under the light of the angry moon." He sat still as granite in the dark house, but Ash could see the haunted look in his eyes. The room smelled of sour sweat.

Palak rested one hand on her energy weapon, her finger near the trigger.

"I'm dead already," said the man. "I've failed my mission, and I will never be free of this curse."

Ash leaned against the far wall, her posture a perfect imitation of the casual observer, even though every instinct in her body told her that what she was hearing would change everything. "What curse?"

Kett fixed his yellow eyes on her. He seemed to weigh her by some measure. A quick glance to

Hector and Palak, and they were dismissed. When he spoke again, it was directly to Ash. "My people bear a terrible curse. The anger, the fear. It eats us from inside and consumes the very soul. This is the way of my people, and we have survived this for generations.

"They sent me to learn more about your kind. When I saw how many people lived here, I understood the threat you would pose, and I communicated that to them. I decided to mingle on the outskirts of town in order to learn more of your customs and discern your strange ways."

Palak said, "So, you're a scout for the invaders?"

"We all are what we are," said Kett. "We are the monsters who stalk the dead lands at night. We live by the broken sea and feed off fear and blood."

"That's a pretty creepy answer, Kett," said Ash.

Kett returned his piercing gaze to her. "Could I be anything else to you?"

Ash took a step forward and peered at the big man. With time to pause and observe, she saw the clear markers that she associated with the Skylings: fleshy ridges along the nose, a modified mouth with sharp teeth, and vicious claws. "You're clearly different from the baseline humans from Earth," she said. When he didn't look like he understood, she explained, "You must be from another colony. But you don't look like the people from the ship. You look like some of the children we have in our colony. We call them Skylings, but the eldest of them is only a few years old."

Kett winced, as if in pain. "To bestow the blessing to a child is a terrible thing. Maybe I am not the only monster here."

"Blessing?"

"One and the same with the curse."

Ash said, "You hurt my friend."

Kett flashed an expression of anger. "Your friend is as good as dead, but it is nothing compared to what you've done to us."

Palak tensed. "And what would that be?"

The man closed his eyes, and for the span of several breaths, Ash wasn't sure he would speak. "One day long ago the skies changed, raining death upon our people. For a year it rained what was known as the soilstorm."

"We call it a blossom storm," Ash said, "but soil-storm's not bad."

"The storm rained filth upon our whole world. It soured our lands and poisoned the sea. For days the rains came, and the muck choked our meager crops and killed our livestock. The poisons brought a blight upon our people, and the elders decided we must retreat farther back into the caves."

Ash decided not to mention that her atmosphere-scrubbing microorganisms caused the storms. Maybe she could bring that up later.

"Then, as we retreated to our underground city, we saw the colors light up the night sky. Great explosions high atop the mountain cliffs. The sky burned orange and pink and red."

"The fireworks," Ash said. "On the night we met Anvil."

"We knew then that there must be someone building something dangerous up atop the mountain. This force needed to be dealt with before it destroyed us all.

"The ritual bestows us both blessing and curse. It grants the ability to breathe the poisonous air and it grants health and strength. I was chosen to venture up the mountain so that I might scout these areas. I climbed the mountain, making my way into the skies above.

"I warned my people about you, but soon discovered my mistake. Your town is not a terrible war machine, but a simple settlement of scholars and scientists. I attempted to approach, but they saw what the blessing had made me. By then, my face had changed, but my claws were not in. They told their children to fear me. *They* feared me, and their fear fed the monster inside me.

"Then, the night came when the angry moon shone and I could not find shelter. I-I must have blacked out. In fear for what I might have done, I fled with nothing. I grew hungry, but I followed a giant walking machine on its way to this settlement. The thing carried people and supplies, and when I discovered how big this place was and the strange dress of its people, I knew I could walk unrecognized in the streets under cover of a hood or mask.

"For a while, it worked. I spoke with people who

thought I was from a pyramid. I learned a little of your ways and saw how you produced food with your machines. It was good. For a while, all was good."

Ash said, "But you started attacking people."

"The curse eats at me, and it was all I could do not to be consumed by rage at the sight of the angry moon. This place has stripped my hold on civilization, and I become wilder with every passing day. Soon I could no longer walk among the people of this area, but it mattered not. People knew a monster lived here at the edge of town. They did not know how right they might be."

"Why is the moon angry?" Ash asked.

Kett's brow furrowed. "Yaz is the moon from which all anger flows."

"So, it's like a religious thing?"

"It is the truth."

"But moons just reflect radiation from the sun," Ash said. "Why would Yaz be any different?"

Palak held up a hand to stop Ash. "What happened then? Did you call for the attack? How many people do you have in your army?"

Kett said, "Without my return at the appointed time, my people assumed I had perished. They sent more to raid the town that I had described in my initial reports."

"So that's all it is. Greed?" Palak said.

"We are starving," Kett growled.

"The attack was more than a raid," Palak spat. "It

was a massacre. Your people are violent monsters and they killed innocents. Children."

"Would you really eat people?" Ash asked.

Kett's mouth turned down in a deep frown. "I would consider it."

Palak tensed.

Ash held out a hand. "Wait, Palak."

Kett's raspy breaths grew louder and deeper. He locked his gaze on Palak and slowly, with great effort, stood against the far wall. Fury bubbled beneath in his hooded yellow eyes. "We are what we are, young one. We do what we must to survive this horrid world. We *become* what we must." His muscles tensed. He towered taller than Palak—taller even than Hector. Ash hadn't realized he was so big. How had she ever escaped his attack? "Our childhoods are lived in secluded places deep beneath the mountain. Only the rite of the blessing allows us to live under the open sky. For generations we've lived this way, and we were content." His voice rose from a snarl to a shout. "It was you who attacked us. It was *you* who destroyed our peace. *You* who are consumed in greed."

Palak raised her weapon, but Ash took a step between them. Ash cast a warning glance at Hector, and he stood at the ready.

"I want to know more about this blessing," Ash said.

Kett's voice was a wet rumble. "Our children are like yours, soft and weak. When we reach adulthood, we can choose to undergo the transformation. It lets us live in the outside world and breathe the air. But it comes at a cost."

"It makes you crave human flesh," Ash said before she could stop herself.

Kett snarled. "Change burns our very souls. It consumes us in the crucible of our bodies and what comes out is something new."

"Like a butterfly," Ash said.

Kett clenched his fists. "A what?"

"It's an insect from Earth. It would start out all soft and squishy, then it wrapped itself up into a cocoon, turned into mush, and then came out as this big winged thing."

Hector chuckled. "Like a bat."

"No, not like a bat," said Ash. "They were more colorful than bats."

"I think I read about them," said Hector. "They had gigantic beaks that were good for cracking nuts and crushing mice."

Kett said, "What—"

"That's a toucan," said Ash. "Butterflies are smaller than that and they're an insect. Like a spider."

"Spiders aren't insects," Hector said. "Everybody knows that."

Palak lowered her weapon. "What are you two even talking about?"

"Butterflies," said both Hector and Ash at once.

"Like our friend here," said Ash, waving a hand

at Kett. "He's in the mush stage, and his body is undergoing changes. They probably have a way to stabilize the change. I thought that was obvious from what he was saying." She didn't say that it was obvious from the mutations of his face, which she thought was rather tactful of her. "He's ugly, but still changing." Moderately tactful.

"Strong like a butterfly," Hector said. "Hence the comparison."

Palak shook her head. "How do you know what he's saying is true?"

"Look at him," Ash said. "He's clearly turning into some kind of butterfly man."

Kett's breathing rasped like the sharpening of a blade.

Palak stepped up beside Ash and raised her weapon. "His people are going to attack, and he knows everything about us. He's too dangerous to keep alive."

"What?" Ash asked, appalled. "How do you get that idea?"

"He's been collecting information on us for months."

"But he's just a guy looking for food on a mostly lifeless planet."

"Yeah," Palak snarled, "and we're the food. We'll live in fear as long as his people are out there."

"Palak—"

Palak raised her weapon.

Ash shoved Palak's weapon aside as she fired. A burning hot bolt of power seared past Kett's head.

Kett lunged.

Hector intercepted the monster. The two men crashed into the wall, and the house's structure cracked under the force. Hector changed direction and threw Kett to the floor.

Palak brought her weapon around to him, but Ash grabbed hold of the searing-hot barrel and shoved. Palak pulled the trigger, but it hadn't recharged. The shot fizzled.

Kett grabbed Ash's ankle.

"I'm trying to help you," Ash said through gritted teeth.

"Let her kill me," the man rasped. "This only gets worse for me." He gripped tighter. "For anyone touched by the curse."

Palak pulled hard on the weapon, yanking Ash from Kett's grip.

Hector dropped onto Kett, pinning him in place.

"Stop," Ash said to Palak.

Palak lowered her weapon. "They murdered our people," she whispered. "Ate them."

Ash said, "But it wasn't him."

"The science committee will bury this," Palak said. "They bury everything."

Ash clenched her jaw. Palak was right. If they brought Kett directly to Olympia, they'd be cut from the conversation. "You don't know that."

"They knew what was coming, Ash. I'm sure of

it." Palak stalked from the little house, leaving the door open so the searing daylight burned into Ash's skull. She winced as the powerful headache returned with full force.

Kett cast his pleading eyes up at her. "Please..."

Ash said to Hector, "Lock him up in the old jail-house." She picked up Mr. Floofers's case from the table and stalked out into the blazing sun.

CHAPTER EIGHT

HECTOR LET out the sigh that meant he was done arguing. It was the rare limit of his tolerance, and Ash was surprised to have reached it so early in the morning.

"It worked last week." Ash *hated* dark blue, and after a week of wearing it, she was ready to hack through Traverse's fashion firewall once again.

"It'll help us fit in."

"Why does that even matter? Why is Traverse using color to label us?"

"Dark blue isn't so bad." He'd used that argument no fewer than seven times already and based on the burnt orange he wore the point held up fairly well.

"Fine," Ash said. She programmed a pointedly drab outfit for herself. Formless navy dress with a matching scrunchie for her hair. While it printed, she flopped on the bed next to Hector and nestled in so she could rest her head on his shoulder.

"How's the wall?" Mr. Floofers climbed on her belly. His warm little body rose and fell as she breathed.

Hector's shrug jostled her head. "It feels good to build something again."

"What if bad guys go over it?"

"It'll be tall."

"Under?"

"Solid rock."

"Through." She mimed a monster crashing through a wall, disturbing Mr. Floofers.

He chuckled. "What are you making? Deadly pathogens?"

"That's so inelegant. I can do way better than that." When he didn't laugh, she said, "Relax, I have no interest in biological warfare. I'm not really comfortable with any of this."

"I know."

"Building weapons leads to people making excuses to use weapons."

He whispered, "You're not supposed to talk about that when Traverse is listening."

"I turned the audio nodes off in here."

Hector sat up, sending Mr. Floofers scurrying away and Ash flopping over on the bed. "How did you do that?" A hint of nervousness crept into his voice.

"With my tablet."

"Rumor was, it was stolen."

"It *was* stolen. I have it back now."

Hector scowled. "Is it true that when Olympia asked for it, you said you didn't have it?"

She splayed her fingers out in a broad gesture of revelation. "I *lied*."

He grumbled disapproval, but the printer dinged so Ash hopped up. Her dress was comically, ironically bland. Its flat form fit her like a garbage bag with the arms cut out and was almost as flattering.

"Have fun building your wall!" Ash called as she dashed out the door. She wasn't sure a wall would really help, but it seemed to make Hector happy, and that was good enough. It bothered to see him on edge.

Her own help with the defense, though, might be more useful.

"What do you mean, *instant banquet*?" Jasper asked when she approached him with the idea in the biolab.

Ash shifted to his other side of his station to avoid being seen by Olympia. No need to get her involved in this, especially when Ash still had the tablet. "It'll be stored full of food that can be instantly deployed. If the attackers are hungry, they'll be attracted to that instead of, um, eating people."

"Eating people?" Jasper exclaimed. "They eat *people*?"

Ash felt her attempt at a peaceful solution slipping somewhat. "Only because they're hungry."

"How did you learn they were hungry?" Jasper didn't know about Kett, and neither did most of the residents of Edge. She had visited the monster every day for a week, and he still hadn't given her any more information.

"Can your plants grow fast enough to make this work?"

He tugged at the too-short sleeves of his burgundy scrubs. "I don't think I can justify this as a defense project."

"Just do it, though."

"Everything goes through committee now. With our problems with computing, hardly anything gets done these days. The lab printers barely function, so how do you think I'm going to produce an instant feast for our visiting friends?"

"Banquet."

"Sure," he drolled. "Banquet. It's not a good plan, Ash."

Olympia crossed the lab, and Ash had to reposition again so she wasn't seen. She wouldn't get anything from Jasper. That much was clear. The botanist was her best bet for having the skills to produce volatile aromatic substances, but maybe she could talk to Leonard the chemist or even Gerald.

"Juliette can help you," Jasper said as Ash walked away.

"Food science!" Ash exclaimed. Because, of course.

Juliette bustled around her lab in the exquisitely equipped and fully functional foodlab. The building had been built into the cliffside over a particularly gloomy section of Edge, where it could distribute the products of its experiments to the hungry people living below. When Ash first found her way into the shining, perfect lab, she couldn't help but take a few minutes to marvel at its neat efficiency.

"Your computers work!" she exclaimed as she swiped through several menus without even a single glitch.

Juliette slapped her hand with a long spoon. "You're not authorized."

"I took a class on food theory back on the ship," Ash said.

"You did," said Juliette, "and you decided that food science was a joke, so you moved on to something less practical."

"Biology is a pretty big deal."

Juliette raised a skeptical eyebrow. "I thought you did microbiology."

"I branch out."

"Is this a hobby to you?" Juliette used the spoon to stir a boiling pot of brown sauce that smelled like salt and cardamom.

Ash gave the question more serious consideration than it deserved, and all she came up with was, "Maybe?"

That stopped Juliette. "Do you get paid for it?"

"Yes."

"Then it's not a hobby. It's a job." She looked Ash up and down. "And it appears as if you're not doing it."

"Everyone's working on defense, so I'm helping with that."

Juliette crossed the expanse of her huge kitchen lab and punched some commands into the food printer. "You people have asked before and the answer is still no."

"Asked what?"

"You can't take over foodlab. Our systems still work because we're more careful with them. If you take over, we won't be able to produce enough food to fill and satisfy the whole population." She fixed Ash with a steady gaze. "Do you understand why that's important?"

Ash bowed her head. "I'm not here to take over your lab." It was a pretty good idea, though. She started thinking about all the ways she could try to gain a foothold. Leonard, the chemist, had somehow secured a place in biolab, and that had led to all kinds of cross-contamination. "I have an idea that you can help with."

The plump woman flashed a grin as if expecting the punch line of a joke.

"They're hungry. The attack on Anvil happened because they needed food."

"Palak's report sounded a lot more violent than a raid for food. Angrier."

Ash swatted the comment away. "Nobody gets that angry. They're hungry, and maybe their instinct tells them that we're food. I want something that smells like delicious people, but way stronger."

Juliette's jaw tightened. "You want me to make a meal of people."

"More like people concentrate." Ash sniffed at the pot of brown liquid. "*Imitation* people concentrate. A whole banquet of it."

"A people banquet." Juliette shooed Ash away from the pot. "And we're just going to set it up at the edge of town?"

"Let me worry about deploying it. If we can negotiate peace, then maybe we don't need weapons at all. Don't you think that sounds better than what everyone else has planned? Palak is making spears and guns. Leonard is making explosive projectiles and pretending like they're fireworks. Jasper's laser turrets—"

"Don't tell me about Jasper."

"I'm sorry." Ash remembered too late that Juliette and Jasper used to be a couple. Now Jasper was with Gerald, and Juliette—Ash supposed she was probably still alone. "It's just that they're all designing solutions that are violent and deadly, but what if there's a peaceful solution?"

"You were at the committee meeting, Ash. We're up against monsters."

"All the monsters I've ever met have been people," Ash said.

"That's horrifying."

"And true." Ash pushed a couple buttons on the console, and Traverse's logo spun. "I don't need much from you right now. Just give me a list of the different synthetic flavors you can make and maybe print a sample of each for me."

"First of all, there are millions. Second of all, no way am I doing that for you." Juliette gently nudged Ash from the screen as a list of potential flavors popped up. "Third of all, what good will that do you? You'd need a test subject, in case the monster's preferences are different from ours."

Ash opened her mouth to respond, but there wasn't anywhere the conversation could go that wouldn't reveal to Juliette that she had a member of team monster holed up in the old jailhouse. "I have to go," she said, quite convincingly, and on her way out the door, shouted back, "Just get that sampling for me by tonight, thanks!"

On her way out of the foodlab, she ran into the man she had met after the monster attack. He still wore the same top hat and black suit, which somehow had avoided becoming wrinkled or dirty. When she approached, he looked up and hid a frayed thread sticking out of his sleeve.

"Ludolf!" she cried. wrapping him up in a hug.

The man went completely stiff. "Hello, Ash Morgan," he said as he extracted himself from her exuberance. He smoothed the front of his suit.

She gestured for him to walk with her, "How are you settling in?"

"They gave me a room to live in."

"Comfy, right?"

"There were some colonists with weapons just now. I think they were training."

Ash frowned. "If you want to help with the defense, I'm sure Hector could use some help building his wall."

Ludolf hugged himself against a cool wind. "I don't think that will be a good use of my skills. I would like to join the guards if they'll take me, but building walls isn't something I can easily do."

"Sometimes we need to adapt. I'm working with the food scientists."

His brow furrowed. "Food science?"

"That's what I said! Food isn't really a science. It's just cooking."

He stopped walking. "Food is sacred."

Ash turned to face the man in the busy street, but when she opened her mouth to respond she saw he wasn't looking at her. His attention was focused on a small group farther down the narrow cobblestone path where Allan the caretaker worked with several others to corral a dozen small children. The first Skyling, Skye, was the largest, and he played with Olympia's three daughters. Allan also carried two smaller ones.

Ash felt a pang of guilt. She still hadn't visited Skye, and seeing him now sent an ache through her heart. He was so big. So different. "They're good kids."

Ludolf said nothing until the group moved away.

ANTHONY W. EICHENLAUB

He drew in several deep breaths. "What will they be when they grow up?"

Ash knew this one. "Adults."

He shot her a questioning look. "Have you considered their nature? They have claws and sharp teeth. These're predators by nature, and they're not equipped to overcome that."

A guinea pig scurried across Ash's feet. "This place could use a few more predators. Anyway, they can grow up to be whatever they want, but I can't imagine anyone wanting to be anything other than a microbiologist."

"What about food science?"

"It's a lesser science."

Ludolf chewed on his lower lip. "This place has me on edge, and I don't know if I'll ever feel safe."

Ash looked to the Commons, then to the outer settlements. "See those buildings over there?" She pointed at the newly built dormitories. "Those are where they're training guards." She pointed to the biolab. "They're making biocorrosive acid-spitters over there, and here in the Commons they're putting together a kind of pulse sound weapon that will stun and disable whoever it hits."

"That's all very serious."

"Plus, Hector is building a wall."

Ludolf raised an eyebrow. "What good will a wall do?"

"It'll keep Hector busy." She thought of him attached to the machine in Pyramid, where he helped

86

so many people but couldn't do anything for himself. "If we're lucky it'll make him happy again." Ash slapped Ludolf's shoulder, ignoring his flinching. "Come find me if you want a drink, but right now I need to figure out how to break into a hospital."

CHAPTER NINE

"I'm not cutting a hole in the roof of the Commons," said Hector from atop the roof of their little barnacle house as the sun set over the bustling city below.

Ash pointed at the building. "Right under that emitter thing."

"You don't even know what that thing does."

"Sure I do. It beams molecules out that bind with the particulates in the air so that we can"—she drew a deep breath through her naked nose—"breathe without strapping on a rebreather."

"And that makes you mad because..."

Ash grumbled, "It's a solution I hadn't thought of." She perked up. "I just need a *little* hole."

"You said you wanted it to be big enough for you to sneak in."

"I'm little," she sulked.

He let out an enormous and dramatic sigh. "You

had to know I wouldn't go for that plan. Why do you want to visit Simon, anyway?"

"We can go underneath. There's sewer systems, and—"

"We're not going through the sewers."

"But—"

"I've been down in the access tunnels. It's not someplace you go for fun."

"This isn't for fun. I need to know what's happening with Simon. It's been a whole week."

"Can you repeat for me what your initial argument was for this? Because I forgot."

Ash whispered, "'Come on. It'll be fun.'"

"What's that?" But this time, Ash caught a hint of amusement in his voice.

"I said it'll be fun, and I meant it." She lay back on the roof to let the last rays of the setting sun wash over her. "Everything's different, Hector."

"You're just upset that nobody built a statue of you for all your amazing deeds."

Ash pouted, "It wouldn't have to be any more than quadruple life-size."

He reached over and took one of her hands in his. "My old construction crew doesn't get together for drinks anymore."

"All the food tastes funny." She slid her butt closer to him so she could rest her head on his shoulder.

"You're still upset that food science is considered real science."

"I'm not!" She considered it. "Mostly. Juliette said she'd get me a dozen samples to test on Kett tomorrow night."

"I don't get this gatekeeping scientists do. Everyone thinks their science is the best and every other science is fake, but everyone's discipline is clearly dependent upon everyone else. Why work so hard to keep others out?"

"I am *not* dependent upon food science."

"Weren't you always talking about how your microbiome could be used to fine tune the nutritional inputs and outputs of any living organism on the planet?"

"Well, I..." Ash stopped midsentence and reconsidered. "Wait, you were listening?"

"I thought there might be a quiz."

"The biolab is basically shut down," Ash said. "They still work, but everyone has to do math by hand so hardly anything gets done."

"They don't let people drive construction spiders in town anymore," complained Hector. "It's all designed on screen and built by automated drones."

Ash twisted around so she could look him right in the eyes. She saw a pain there that she'd never noticed before. Hector had always built things, and now the job he'd loved no longer existed. The push for efficiency had forced the colonists to move to the more automated approach. "Sounds like we're both unemployed."

"Might as well turn to a life of crime."

"So how are we going to get into that hospital room?"

"Probably just ask nicely."

Ash scoffed, "Tried that. Didn't work."

"Olympia promised to let us in if you give back that tablet."

"Nope."

"It'd be an easy way to get in. And then the scientists in the lab will get more work done."

"They'll use it for evil."

"Ash, come on. That tablet hardly even works anymore."

Ash sat up and pulled the tablet from her pocket. It worked fine, even though a spider web of cracks prevented a quarter of the touchscreen from registering properly.

Hector sighed. "Well, maybe you can leverage that into a new job."

The dark sky still held the last lingering blues of the dying sunset. Ash pushed a few buttons on the tablet and brought up a satellite view of Edge. "This place has grown so much," she said. "It's changed everything around it."

"They built homes in the quarry and made a new quarry farther out. There's a second reservoir now."

Ash zoomed in on the reservoir. "Can you believe they let people swim in it?"

Hector sat up and peered at the screen. "You know, the bigger we get, the more impact we have on the land. We shape it, whether we try to or not."

Ash zoomed out again and looked at the city as a whole. "What did Kett say about his village?"

"Seaside," Hector said, leaning back. "But he didn't say where it was."

"Sure, but look." Ash showed Hector the land where the Anvil colony stood. "Look at these straight lines. Look at the way this granite is exposed. Traverse's sky view edits out the colony itself, but it still shows us the shape of the land around it."

Hector scratched his chin. "Kett said that they saw the skies light up with color. That had to refer to the time we set off fireworks near Anvil."

"Then they're able to see the sky over Anvil." She circled an area of a few dozen miles along the coast.

"What would you look for, though?"

Ash zoomed in close to the shoreline. "Suspicious stuff."

"Those little islands look like a face," Hector said after the sky was dark and the air grew cold. "It looks like Leonard, actually.'

She turned the tablet to get a better look. It really did look like Leonard, complete with an unruly mess of hair. "Maybe one of the old settlements predicted the rise of Leonard."

"Well, there's a clone of him from Pyramid, isn't there? Maybe there's an eternal line of Leonards going back to the dawn of Sky."

Ash zoomed closer to the picture. "And then, to appease their Leonard, they crafted an image of his face out of stone, carving it away over generations so that it would look exactly like ocean-worn granite."

"It seems unlikely," Hector deadpanned.

"Indeed." Ash continued down the coast.

Shouting rose from the city below, but Ash couldn't tell if it was anger or excitement. There were games happening in the arena attached to the Commons, and clusters of five to ten spectators wandered their way drunkenly through the center of town.

"I keep seeing straight lines," Ash said, "but I think that's the natural form of the granite when it breaks."

"Should we bring in a geologist?"

"Junk science," Ash spat. She moved on.

As three moons rose like ghosts over the tops of the colony's tallest buildings, Ash finally saw it. An indentation along the cliffside stretched for several miles in a perfect semicircle. Stones in the shallows formed an oblong crescent, which would provide protection from the ocean's relentless waves. In the nook nearest the cliff, a long, perfectly straight line ran counter to the angular lines of the naturally broken stone.

"That might be something," Ash admitted. "I should go check it out."

Hector pressed his lips together.

"You're right," Ash sighed. "I think I've had enough travel for at least a few more weeks."

"We should show this to Olympia," Hector said.

"Tomorrow," said Ash.

"Why not right now?"

"Also, not Olympia."

"Ash."

"She'd never give back my tablet! Plus, I promised Palak I would bring information to her first. The science committee will hide this."

"Will she listen to you on something like this?"

Probably not. "She definitely will."

"Fine." His tone indicated that it was *not* fine, but he didn't press the issue.

———

THE NEXT EVENING, after a dreadfully boring day of grilling Kett in the jailhouse without gaining any useful information, visiting the hospital only to find Simon was still on lockdown, visiting Olympia only to learn that she *still* wouldn't let them talk to Simon, and fiddling around in the biolab with an absolute failure to engage in anything productive, they met in front of the tall buildings where Palak's army practiced. Ash watched for several minutes as a scraggly group of mostly Pyramidians practiced with light fiber spears.

"Olympia's been telling the med staff to keep us away from Simon," said Ash. "But I overheard that he's going home today."

"Overheard?"

Ash mumbled, "Broke into a secure comm feed."

Hector's jaw tightened.

"I mean, what is she hiding? I could have helped."

"Your help—"

"Don't even give me all that nonsense about my help actually causing more harm than good. He signed a waiver every single time."

Palak spotted Ash. "Coming here to train?"

"I have some information."

Palak waved her over. Hector followed.

"We'll want to check it out in person," Ash said after showing Palak the find. "We could send delegates down to see if someone's really there. If they exist, we introduce ourselves the same way we did with Anvil."

"With fireworks and a kraken?"

"In peace. It's the only way to diffuse this whole thing."

Palak rolled her eyes. "The time for peace is gone, Ash. They killed a lot of our people, and if this is where they live, then we need to strike as fast as possible."

"You need to take this to the science committee."

"They won't listen."

Ash pointed at the screen. "They listen to facts, and they'll listen to you."

Palak folded her arms. "They will listen because we will tell them what we have already done." Behind her, the Pyramidians shouted in unison as they ran through their drills. "That is what it means to be in charge of defense."

"Attacking another colony isn't defense."

Palak rolled her eyes. "You were always too soft, Ash."

"I'm the only one with a solution that doesn't get anyone killed."

Palak thumped the butt of her spear on the hard earth. "What makes you think they can even negotiate?"

"Kett seemed reasonable enough."

"He also said he would consider eating us."

"But not that he *preferred* it."

"They're monsters. They rolled in from the rocks and killed our people. Tore them to shreds. Then they fled into the wastes, back to their home."

"Kett isn't a monster."

"He attacked you."

"But he feels bad about it."

Palak rolled her eyes again. "Whatever's left of this settlement you're talking about isn't human enough to worry about. You saw Kett. He's a monster. The rest of them are people who will turn into monsters. We need to strike them and destroy them before they attack again.'

"Kett could help. We can bring him with."

Palak threw her hands in the air and turned away. "When the next attack comes, we're going to need a way to strike at where *they* live. We need to force them to back down. *Then* we can negotiate."

Ash bit back a retort. Instead, she said, "Please, Palak. We can be better than this."

"We've never been better than this." Palak paused at the doorway to the barracks. "Thanks. For bringing this to me."

"I'm coming with," Ash said.

Hector placed a hand on Ash's shoulder. "Ash, don't—"

Palak turned away. "No."

A heavy silence settled over them as a hazy moon watched down between black towers. For a long time, Ash didn't know how to move forward, as if time itself was stuck. She'd stay there forever waiting for the right words to emerge that would convince Palak to step back from her vendetta.

"You know I'm right," Ash finally said.

"Right doesn't mean anything these days," Palak said. "Maybe it never did."

"Come on, Ash," Hector said. "Let's go."

Ash pulled away from him and pursued Palak into the building. "Take full breather masks. The seaside air is poisonous."

Palak clenched her jaw. "We'll leave in the morning." Her knuckles went visibly white. "This is how we win. We need to be willing to strike back."

Ash pulled her comm unit and touched it to Palak's. "I'll send a chain of crawlers after you to connect a signal so that we can stay in touch."

Palak studied the map on her screen. "Half of my army is already in Anvil. I'm taking the rest with me."

"That'll leave Edge defenseless," Hector said.

Palak scoffed, "There are proton cannons on every city block. There's a laser mounted atop the Archives. Anybody can pick up an energy weapon and defend this place." She gestured in the direction of her troops. "What I'm training here is a strike force. Trust me, this is how wars end."

"This doesn't sound like a war ending," Ash said.

"You have to strike at the heart to slay a monster, and if they attack Edge, they'll be decimated."

"They're not monsters."

"You always have to make things hard, don't you?" Palak put her screen away with a look of distaste. She looked up at the doorway, where Hector's giant form was a silhouette in the moonlight. She bent down and opened a chest at her feet, revealing a dozen long-barreled energy weapons like the one strapped to her back. "The rules are changing, Ash. You've been gone awhile, so you've probably noticed the big stuff, but there are other things too. Traverse is letting us make the weapons we designed. We can make more of these."

Ash took a step back. "No."

"I think Traverse has plans for us."

"When have its plans ever worked in our favor?"

Palak looked up from where she crouched next to the chest. "They always do until they don't."

"I could have told you that ages ago."

A wry smile tugged at the corner of Palak's lips.

"You have no idea how hard it is to listen to you when you're right."

Outside, as Ash and Hector walked away from the barracks and Palak's small army, Ash said, "We should have gone straight to Olympia."

Hector took her hand in his and said, "She's probably home by now. We could pay her and Simon a friendly visit."

A wide grin spread across Ash's face. "If Simon's really home, maybe they'll give us blood samples."

"You have an interesting concept of what makes a friendly visit."

CHAPTER TEN

Ash wore her black leather coat over dark-blue scrubs and moved with Hector through the darkening streets. The sun had set and the black towers over Edge stood sentinel against the backdrop of the approaching moons.

Olympia and Simon lived in a compact two-level, with large bay windows on the upper floors that over-looked the ocean. It stood near the edge of town, set far enough downslope that it still had unencumbered views of both the top of the Commons dome and the massive arch that marked the new outer limit of the colony.

"How is your wall coming?" Ash asked when she saw the arch.

Hector mumbled, "It's not done yet."

Far away, revelers whooped in joy at some fantastic adventure in the city. Lights along the streets upslope glowed fiercely, consuming the stars in a wash of white. It all felt strange to Ash, and she ached for the small colony she had left so long ago.

Hector pointed to the house's back door, where the shadows clung to the face of the house. A figure left the house and crept along the edge of the open road, sticking to the darkened corners.

"That might be Simon," Hector whispered.

"It could be Olympia. She's sneaky like that, and she might be trying to draw us out."

"Olympia is the least sneaky person I know, and I thought you came here to speak with her."

"I'll follow for a while and see what they do." She tapped her comm unit. "You go tell Olympia about the Seaside colony."

"What?" Hector whispered. "I'm not going to tell her."

"She needs to know."

"Are you kidding? First thing she's going to ask is where you are and where's the proof. No way am I going—"

Ash shushed him.

He stared at her, aghast until she planted a kiss on his cheek. The tension melted out of him, but he held out one of his big hands. Ash reluctantly handed him the tablet.

She set out after the shadowy figure, who had already put some distance between them. Allowing for the space of several large buildings, Ash stayed just close enough to watch the figure move through the city. It was a dangerous distance, but three moons hung high in the sky and the streetlights spattered the pavement with pools of light. Simon—if it was indeed Simon—worked his way through the shadows very carefully and remained difficult to see.

They moved closer to the center of town, where the Pyramidians had set up something like an entertainment district. As they made their way through the shadows, they passed more and more midnight revelers. When they neared a particularly bright section of street, the shadow stood straight, pulled the hood back from his head, and walked into the crowd.

It was Simon, but Ash was shocked at the sight of him. The bones of his already narrow face showed through sallow skin. His beard—normally a wispy, light thing—clung to his chin like a dark shadow. And his hair, usually the prettiest hair Ash had ever seen, sat thick against his skull, clinging to his forehead with grease and sweat. This was the worst Ash had ever seen her friend, and she'd seen him badly injured before.

This was something else.

He stepped quickly through the crowd. Music thumped in the distance, and Ash recognized the asynchronous rhythms of the late twenty-first-century Earth. Earth retro fashion emerged in the crowd, all rendered in the monochromes. Women wore swooping capes and billowing sleeves, their bodies lost in a sea of cloth and comfort. Men stood tall and proud in tight suits tailored to absolute perfection.

Ambiguously gendered people wore flowing suits that captured the essence of both and brought its own pocket-laden practicality to the mix. Ash passed a musician playing a ten-string guitar, and she wanted nothing more than to listen to his mournful renditions of the early twentieth-century blues.

Simon disapproved up ahead. She rushed after him, pushing past strangers as she worked her way uphill. Twisting passages through tall buildings left her confused and disoriented. She could no longer tell which direction was upslope or which led to the ocean view.

Bright signs promised music and drinks and fun. They blazed like a thousand suns into the night, making daylight of the late hours. The insides of those same establishments were inky shadows, swallowing revelers who wandered too close to their dangerous maws.

She reached out and grabbed Simon's arm.

He spun on her and blinked. For a fraction of a second, Ash saw Kett's eyes in Simon's face. The flecks of gold flashed in the too-bright lights as he focused on her.

Then, a smile spread across his gaunt face. "Ash, it's good to see you."

Ash caught a whiff of something delicious and led Simon to a stand where someone was selling vegetable skewers. She bought two of them and handed one to her friend. "Here. Now we're even for all the times you paid for my drinks. What are you doing out here?"

He looked down at the food in his hands and sniffed it cautiously. "I couldn't sleep."

They found a bench to sit on when a group of Anvilites wandered away. Ash took a bite from the skewer. It had a complex, spicy flavor like nothing she'd ever tried. The taste lingered. "We tried to visit you in the hospital."

"I know," he said. He scratched the bridge of his nose, where, up close, Ash could see a rash bubbling at the surface of his skin. "This infection is really messing with me."

"I'm a biologist."

He watched a group of teens in lavender kimonos wander past. "I feel restless."

"I could probably help," Ash said. "I mean, I at least could try to isolate the microbe of the infection. Not that the med techs are bad at that or anything. I don't want to cast any doubt on what they're doing." She considered it for a moment. "Although they told me there wasn't a microbe. What kind of crackpot medical system do we have around here these days?"

"You know when you're really hungry for one specific thing?" He looked down at the skewer with disgust. "But you don't know what that thing is."

Ash bit a mushroom off of hers and spoke through a full mouth. "The food actually got better while I was gone. Don't let Juliette know I said this, but food science really has made some good progress."

"It's mostly imported ideas from Pyramid."

"I knew it."

A couple of Pyramidians wandered by, their smooth, deep accents strange against the raucous, drunken fury of the night. Simon peered at them, face impassive. He clutched one hand to his chest where he must have still had bandages under his clothes. "I don't think I should be here." He tilted his head up to peer at the sky. They sat in the shadow between two pools of bright streetlights, but the ambient glow still obscured their view of the moons above. "You should probably leave, Ash."

Ash threw an arm around her friend. "Simon, I just found you. If instinct tells you that it's time to be out on the town, you know I'm going to be there with you. Hector's on his way too. Just give him a few minutes. It'll be just like old times." She ate a pepper from her skewer. There were only a few pieces left, and she was still hungry. She gulped down the last roasted green lumps, tossed the skewer in the nearby recycler, and reached to take Simon's from him. "You don't mind if I..."

Simon growled.

She handed back the skewer, but he let it slip through his hands and clatter to the ground. "Come on, man," she said. She took his arm and pulled him to his feet. "I think we should walk you home."

"No." The look he shot her sent ice down her

spine. It was the look of a predator. The look of Kett just before he pounced. This was the look of violence without anger, and fury without hatred. The cool, vicious intensity of it cut all the way down to the center of her spine and made her drop his arm and take a step back.

Behind him, through the harsh lights of the reveling street, Ash saw a third moon peek over the tall buildings. It shone behind him in a dusty red, its glow casting shadows in a melancholy hue.

Simon's hand moved faster than she could react. He grabbed her wrist and held her close. His eyes met hers and his breaths came in ragged gasps. "I told you—"

Ash twisted her arm and yanked it free. The skin stung where she pulled free of his grasp, and she stumbled back.

His lips pulled back to reveal white teeth. He took a step forward, his intense gaze never leaving her. "I'm sorry—"

She slammed through the Pyramidians, scattering them in a tumult of curses and cries. Simon followed, calling to her. Her heart hammered in her chest.

"Hector, something's wrong!" Ash called into her comm. She got nothing but static in return.

She turned again, not bothering to look back.

Simon called to her, "Ash, wait. I didn't mean it. I'm sorry."

The lights overhead flickered, then flashed double bright.

Blinded, Ash staggered into a dark alley. She crashed forward through the street, hand in front of her to feel her way. Her shoulder bounced painfully off a stone wall, and she caught a glimpse of Simon behind her. Golden flecks flashed in his eyes. He took a step forward. Then another. His eyes focused on Ash like a predator.

Ash was the prey, trapped in a dead end.

The lights above flickered to life. Dim, white light washed over black walls. Ash bumped up against the far wall. She was trapped. Simon took another step forward. Ash's heart thumped in her throat.

It was that night again, when the monster attacked. Stripping away the familiar aspects of civilization left only a raw, exposed monstrosity, even in Simon. Even in Edge.

Here was a man raw and exposed to the base destructive impulses Ash knew lurked inside them all. How could this pure animal rage ever hope to be controlled? What could Ash ever do but run?

But there was nowhere to run.

"Simon," Hector said from the other end of the alley. "Olympia didn't even know you had left."

Simon twitched, but his gaze didn't falter. "I couldn't be there anymore."

Ash opened her mouth to talk him down, but curiosity tugged at her. "Why not?" She could smell stale sweat rolling off of him.

"The Pyramidians have different ways. There are so many of them. Sometimes they get violent." His hands clenched into fists. "Everything's different."

Ash pressed her back against the wall. "I'm sorry, Simon."

"Olympia told me about the attack," Hector said.

He shook his head as if to clear it. "There were three of them. In this alley. I was afraid, Ash. I had Olympia and the kids with me, and we were lost. This city is so big now." His muscles were so tense he trembled. Anger flashed in his eyes, and tears wet his cheeks. "It's so big and everything is so strange."

Hector stepped closer. "We can talk about this at home."

"Stop!" Simon shouted. When Ash flinched, he held his palms out. Blood stained his hands. "I don't know what I'm doing here."

Ash wanted to say something, but the words stuck in her throat. This was her Simon. How could this possibly happen? Simon wasn't a violent guy, but he scared her.

Her mind raced. There were a dozen ways to achieve a change in personality, and she could probably reproduce half of them in a functioning biolab. What she needed was a sample of Simon's blood. Maybe a brain scan. She needed the clue to what had changed him—and some way of changing him back. She needed to study him.

"That's right," Hector said as Simon's breathing

slowed. "We're just going to take a break and get you home."

Panic rose in Simon's eyes. "I can't go back home."

Hector blinked. "Olympia will—"

"The jailhouse," Ash blurted.

Simon cocked his head. "What?"

"You can't arrest him," said Hector.

"We'll take you to the jailhouse. There's someone you can meet there, and if you want, you can stay there until you're feeling better."

His shoulders tensed. "I made them keep me at the hospital because something didn't feel right."

"And Olympia made them finally release you."

Together, they walked through town, with Hector and Simon flanking their friend the whole way.

Ash still felt the sting on her arm from Simon's attack. The sense of betrayal still lingered in that grip. He had been her friend since she came to the planet. She'd never even considered the thought that he might hurt her. As they walked through town, she made sure to cover her arm so that Hector would not see the four bloody scratches Simon's claws had left on her wrist.

CHAPTER ELEVEN

"It's been over a week, Kett. How about a few more details on this blessing of yours?" Ash spoke through the narrow window in the cell door. She wore her long trench coat and fedora, printed in a striking dark blue. She'd had a day with access to Simon's blood, and the scientific dead ends had frustrated her until she wanted to tear the answer out of the big monster.

Kett sat in the corner of the dark cell, his golden eyes reflecting the narrow slash of light from the window. His voice was the rasp of a razor against stone. "Its scent is on the wind."

Simon sat an arm's length from Ash, chained to the heavy interview table at his own request. The old jailhouse only had one proper cell, and Ash wouldn't lock him in with the monster. Her friend sat with his head down on the table. After the alley, Simon had been repentant, kind, and understanding. For all measures, he seemed to be himself again. He still wanted to be chained up, and he still wouldn't allow Olympia to visit.

"Did you give that tablet back to her?" Simon asked.

"Yes," answered Ash. "But she's still annoyed with both of us."

He rolled his head to one side so he could look at her. "Some things never change."

"Every scan in Traverse's system comes back clean, even when we run it through the tablet. DNA analysis shows no changes. Your blood is normal by any measure I can run through the system." To Kett, she said, "You could have scratched me. You had my ankle when we found you in that house."

Kett smiled, showing his rows of dagger teeth. "It wasn't your time."

She hefted a square case onto the table next to Simon, who now snored gently. She opened it to reveal an angular emitter and more than a dozen biopacks. "I don't think you're as much a monster as you think. Why don't you tell me something about your people?"

Kett drew a deep, rasping breath and closed his eyes. Finally, he said, "My people have lived by the sea for many generations. Poison air has plagued us since the beginning of time."

Ash pressed her face up against the narrow

window so she could get a good look at him. "Tell me about the beginning What is your origin story?" She slotted the first biopack into the emitter and flipped the switch. In a flash of light, the room smelled of oranges and cinnamon. "And tell me if this smells like food to you."

Closing his eyes, Kett drew a deep breath. "The first people descended upon this world as seven perfect humans: three men and three women. The seventh, known as Yaz, was fluid in gender and in all things. They were the wisdom of the Seven, and the source of all truth granted by the god above.

"Many storms passed in those early times. The seven carved their homes into the cliffs with great machines, cutting through stone like the soft fruit of a watermelon."

"Wait. You have melons?" Ash clicked a new biopack into the emitter. It smelled of sour meat. Ash cringed at the smell. Juliette had given her a wide mix, but they weren't all pleasant.

Kett, broken from the intoning of his story, stared at Ash for what seemed like forever.

"It's just that that's an advanced state of agriculture."

Still, he stared.

"Never mind," she said, removing the biopack. "Continue."

"The Seven created our city and bent the world to their will. At night they slept in seven castles built into the cliffside—those same castles that still mark the outer limits of our world. Inside the mountain, they made our homes safe from the poisonous air. In the sea, they built breaks to stop the mighty waves from crushing us even during the storm's full vengeance.

"Many more storms passed, and the seven became longed for more. They wished for children, but the god above told Yaz to forbid the creation of children. They were given many creatures to tend in this world and plants to sow into the soil and ocean.

"Still, the men and women of the Seven were not satisfied. Yaz told them, 'The god above forbids you children until his kingdom is complete, and should you disobey, there will be no end to the storms of his vengeance.' This gave them pause. For several more storms, they toiled in pious duty to their god.

"Then, when the last of the great boroughs was nearly complete, the three men coupled with the three women, and the three women each became pregnant with three children each. The god above was not pleased."

As Kett spoke, Ash cycled through cayenne and nutmeg, basil mint, and something that smelled like the raw tang of fresh blood. None of them elicited any reaction from the monster, though the last one made her stomach twist.

Simon sniffed without opening his eyes. "That one smells good."

Ash called out to Kett, "Is this one irresistibly delicious?"

"Not really," said the monster.

Ash breathed a sigh of relief. "I bet I know where your story's going." If the god above was Traverse, she could imagine what happened next.

"The children were all born strange." Nope, it wasn't that. "Yaz declared that the god above cast them from his sight." That sounded more like it.

Ash pressed closer so she could meet Kett's gaze. "Exactly how strange are we talking?" She fumbled with the next biopack.

"The air outside grew worse. Deadly. Poison flowed from above. Yaz, the wise, told them she had changed their children before they were even conceived. They would be the future of our people. As soon as those children became adults, the Seven would fade away. Their later children would be born normal, but their line would carry a secret heritage.

"The god above would no longer send boons, and the people would suffer for a thousand storms. Our children would live under the mountain, far from the poisonous air, until they became adults. Then, on a day of their choosing, they could accept Yaz's blessing. One scratch from another blessed person would change the new adult into one capable of wandering the world outside."

Ash absently felt at her bandaged wrist. "That's the blessing? A scratch?"

"It starts the change."

"And the curse?"

"Yaz's angry moon causes the changes to progress. The blessed one slowly becomes a monster under their watchful gaze. Our boon of freedom turns the angry moon into a slow curse of death. Those changed as I am are free to go anywhere in this world, but every exposure to the red moon makes them more a monster. Every moment spent a monster brings me closer to death.

"For this reason, the six wished to cast Yaz into the sea, but Yaz expected this response. Yaz created a new citadel upon the angry moon where nobody could reach them. Instead, the six raised their children under the mountain. One day, when the first children had grown into horrible creatures, Yaz returned and called them all out onto the shore. Yaz spoke of promised children that our people would one day find who would lift the curse brought to us through these monsters. The Seven stood once again reunited under Yaz's red moon." Kett looked up with his golden eyes. "Under that moon, the nine were given leave to travel the world in search of the children. The six's new children bore none of the changes of the first generation, but they could not survive long in the world outside, so they lived only underground.

"But when the nine returned with nothing, they bestowed their blessing to the younger generation. And down the generations, whenever a person was to leave the caves or the protected waters, they would first get Yaz's blessing."

"Which would adapt them to the world and then eventually kill them if they stayed out too long."

"Sometimes they return with the most wondrous things." Kett stared at his own hands. "Ancient technology or artifacts of our people from long ago. Sometimes they would find the bones of animals like none we had ever seen or cloth from unknown fibers."

Simon spoke without lifting his head from the table. "We have this story in the Archives."

"Go back to sleep, Simon," Ash said, fiddling with the next biopack in her hand. The label was worn off, and she didn't know what to expect from it. She wrote *Spice Number Six* on the side.

He raised his head. Half of his face was red from where he'd rested on the hard surface. "I'm serious."

"We're talking about Kett's colony. This is a legend that has been passed down generations, so it can't possibly be in the Archives."

Simon licked his dry lips. "Only, our version of the story has seven hundred villagers. Yaz is referred to as Yatz and is known to be the creator of all life who brings perfect children to her people."

"Yatz is God?" Ash asked. "How much truth is in this story?"

Simon looked at her dully. His eyes locked on a glass of water on the table, but he made no move to drink it. Seeing her friend like that made her heart ache. "We never know what truth hides in legends. Maybe none."

Kett said, "It was not seven hundred."

"Fine," said Simon. "It was probably somewhere in between, but the important part is that the adults were earthlings and the children were something like Skylings."

"So, the blessing is like a second puberty," said Ash. Then, the horror struck her. "Oh, I'm sorry, Simon. This is horrible."

He looked at her, aghast. "You didn't think it was horrible before?"

"I mean, rampant morphological changes..."

"I might have killed you if Hector hadn't arrived. Ash, I can't see my family again. If I had been home when the urge hit, I might have hurt the kids."

Kett growled, "The urge is part of our curse. It means the angry moon is making its changes."

"It's not a great feeling," said Simon.

Ash sat across from Simon. She pushed the emitter to one side so she could look him in the eyes. "I'll find a cure," she said.

"There's no cure for puberty," Simon said.

She fingered Spice Number Six. "Once we isolate the problem, we—"

"Is that going to help?" Simon asked, pointing a broken fingernail at her biopack.

Ash held up the cube. "It's an attempt to figure out a delicious smell that will distract the starving outsiders from attacking our people."

"That's ridiculous."

Ash slotted the biopack into the emitter and pressed the button. "Says you."

The effect was almost immediate. Simon jumped back from his seat, snapping his chains hard enough to leave gouges in his wrists. He shouted so loud and so suddenly that Ash flailed in response, sending the emitter crashing across the floor.

Simon let out a guttural cry. "Shut it off!"

Ash, in a panic, dove for the device, but only managed to knock it away. In the other room, Kett let out an anguished cry and crashed hard against the door. It cracked under the force of the blow. Simon bent over double, retching.

Her comm unit crackled to life. Palak's voice came in too loud, "Ash how's our connection?"

Ash swatted at the comm controls, but as she hit the transmit button, Simon let out a frustrated howl.

Kett snarled, "Screaming Yaz, what is that smell?"

The emitter slid under the table. Simon couldn't reach it because of his chains, so he stomped it hard, sending it skittering away from Ash. Tears flowed from his red eyes, and snot flowed from his nose. His body convulsed as he retched.

"It smells like tea," Ash said. It really wasn't bad. A little strong, but—

Simon curled into a ball.

Ash's hand closed around the emitter and she mashed the button. She opened the door to allow fresh air to circulate. Kett let out one last whimpering howl, then settled down in his cell.

"Screaming Yaz?" Ash asked. She popped the biopack out of the emitter and stuffed it in her pocket.

Kett sat against the far wall of his cell. "I apologize for swearing."

Simon stared at her through bleary eyes. "That's not a good one for your welcome banquet."

"I'll file Spice Number Six as a maybe," Ash said.

Simon wiped tears from his red eyes. "File it under potential war crime and we have a deal."

Ash jumped as Palak's voice snapped through the comm. "Is Edge under attack?"

"No, we're fine." Ash turned the volume all the way down. She sat again and took both of his hands in hers. The fingernails had warped and sharpened, and his knuckles showed through too-pale skin. "We'll get through this."

His eyes fixed on her bandaged wrist now exposed. "How bad is your scratch?"

Ash wasn't listening. "Seven," she said.

"W-What?"

"Seven. Both your version and Kett's version use the number seven. That must mean something." She stood, letting the chair topple to the floor behind her. "And the second wave of children seemed like they had a recessive gene. Triggered by what? Triggered by a metal or radiation or a virus? But there wasn't a virus." She crossed the room and peered into Kett's cell. "Was there a virus?"

Kett looked up at her with an expression of pain. "It's the angry moon," he said. "The furious, red moon."

Ash slammed a palm against the door. "That's it!" She rushed from the little jailhouse.

CHAPTER TWELVE

Ash burst into Olympia's office. A dozen video displays showed a dozen rocky terrains across the wide expanse surrounding Edge. "I need it back."

Olympia placed a hand on the tablet, which was wired into the video surveillance system. "Oh, no you don't. This is the only one that we can trust to watch for our enemies."

"Who cares about enemies? I have an idea for a cure."

Olympia raised an eyebrow. "You have a cure? For Simon?"

"I have an *idea* for where to look for the problem, which might lead to a cure."

Olympia traced the logic in the air with one finger. "You don't have anything."

Ash left the office in a huff. She stalked to her lab station, which she'd taken over when she came back. There were enough open stations now, with research grinding to a halt, that she'd had her pick. This one had a nice location next to the window and a whole array of tools Ash had never used before. She yanked out a large scope and pointed it at a sample of Simon's blood. The beam fired, readings clacked through the system and she tried her very best to interpret the results on the screen.

Worthless. Numbers and letters glitched, appearing backwards or upside down. The numbers changed as they scrolled across the screen. The menu system kept selecting options she didn't want, and once when she got all the way into the readout, she found nothing. No virus. No trigger.

Nothing.

But it *couldn't* be nothing. Seven was the key.

She would have to steal that tablet back.

Olympia stepped out of the office, crossed to Ash's station, and said, "Don't even think of stealing that tablet," as she strolled past.

"I wasn't!" Ash called after her. Then to herself, she said, "I wasn't." She totally was, but it no longer felt like a great idea. She needed to let it go.

She couldn't let it go.

Seven. It had to mean something.

Ash pushed open Olympia's unlocked door to look at the video feeds. They spun and moved. Dozens of them, scouring the terrain as automated spider walkers scanned the land for miles around.

"She said you might come," said Tobin. He sat in the dark corner with the light of Ash's screen reflecting in the lenses of his glasses. "I figured you'd wait a bit longer."

"I'm not here to steal the tablet." She had definitely been there to steal the tablet. "I need to look at the videos."

"Oh, that's pretty convincing, Ash. What are you hoping to see on the videos?"

The niggling idea that had been bothering her for the past days finally clicked into place. She pulled up a map of the area. For each video feed, she highlighted a location, direction, and loop of movement. As the last piece emerged, she knew she was right.

"This tablet always tells the truth," she explained, "at least it always lets us know when it's lying."

Tobin stood and leaned over the screen with her. He smelled of sandalwood and mint.

"The same thing happened the other day when I was attacked. Traverse didn't lie about what it saw, but it *did* nudge events so that it wouldn't see anything."

"It made its own blind spots," Tobin said.

Ash pointed to the area on the map not covered by any drones. "Singular," she said. "Blind *spot*."

Tobin's eyes went wide and he sat back down. "I see."

"Traverse," said Ash, "show me what you're not showing me."

The *T* logo spun endlessly on all dozen screens.

"I'm serious, Traverse. I want to see what you haven't been showing me, what you've hidden from the med techs and Olympia. Tell me what nobody here even thought to ask about."

"There's no way this will work," said Olympia walking into the room. "Traverse isn't going to give you anything it doesn't want to."

"It's worse than I thought," said Tobin.

"Hector is making rounds now," Olympia sighed. "We'll have his report on that area soon."

Not soon enough.

"This'll work," Ash said. It wasn't going to work.

"Well, you know how I feel about all this," said Tobin, eyeing Ash's tablet.

"Talk about it in committee for a couple weeks until the problem solves itself?" asked Ash.

"I think every step you're taking brings us closer to the end."

Ash squinted at him. "You think we should ignore the threat?"

"No, but we need to carefully consider how our actions impact our instance of Traverse. It has never allowed the manufacturing of weapons. This could finally break it."

Ash opened her mouth to protest but realized she didn't actually disagree. "We need some way to lure them away without weapons."

"That's right."

"Like some kind of draw that uses their heightened olfactory senses to draw them into someplace where we can calm them and begin negotiations."

"That might work."

"Yes!" Ash flashed him a look of wild brilliance. "That's what I thought." She frowned. "What happens if Traverse is destabilized?"

"We'll need to do what Pyramid did."

"Burn it all to the ground?" A pit of frustration burned in Ash's belly because she knew he might be right. "Destroy Traverse's influence and root it out from all our systems, no matter the consequences?"

Tobin spoke through gritted teeth. "Our reasons were good when we did it in Pyramid, and you're taking this colony to exactly the same situation."

"We're not talking about this right now," Olympia said.

Ash glared at Tobin, and he gave the same back.

"We wait," sighed Olympia. She gestured to the screens, which again showed surveillance footage. "And watch."

Ash opened Olympia's biolab and inserted her samples. One blood sample each of Simon and Kett, one of her own blood, and one sample of Hector, because he was such a supportive guy and volunteered. After several minutes, only the final vial showed signs that Traverse had tested the blood. "Traverse, you're skipping three of the samples, big guy."

"True," boomed Traverse loud enough that Ash flinched.

"Care to explain why?"

Nothing. Ash gathered the samples and carried

them outside, prying carefully at the sealed top of one as she walked.

Tobin followed. "This refusal is typical late Traverse dialogue. Same as we had in Pyramid just prior to the fall."

"Before you crippled your colony by extracting Traverse from every single system." The top popped off the first sample tube. Outside, she took a pinch of soil from under a tuft of golden grass and dropped it in.

"Precisely." Tobin gestured at his perfectly styled self. "And I'm still here to talk about it."

Ash gestured at him wildly with the second sample. "You're here because Hector saved you. Your decaying city would have been your grave if-if..." She blinked fast. It wasn't Tobin's fault nothing worked. There must be something wrong. She pried the top off another sample and sprinkled a pinch of soil in.

"Let me get this straight," said Tobin, calm but smug. "This fancy tablet of yours forces Traverse to tell the truth about what it's seen, so now Traverse actively avoids seeing things that it doesn't want you to know about?"

Ash added soil to the last blood sample and returned to the lab. "Traverse, have you always hidden things like this?"

"Resources are limited."

Tobin continued, "And there's a big gap in the surveillance patrol Olympia set up, meaning a possible army at our doorstep."

Olympia said, "The grid was solid when we programmed it."

"Hector is building a wall," Ash said, lining the samples up in the scanner.

Tobin said, "And your chief of defense's little brigade is off exploring some ruins that you think *might* give us a clue to the history of these monsters?"

As she poked at Traverse's controls, Ash mumbled, "We're undefended, there's an army at our gate, I'm messing around with biological samples trying to get a better reading, we're pretty much all doomed, and it's not my fault."

Olympia gestured at the image of Hector's arch. "The committee didn't authorize any of this."

Ash flinched. "You were busy."

"We do things by committee now," said Tobin. "It's a lesson we learned in Pyramid."

"So, is there really a wall?" asked Olympia. "Some hope that we might deter attackers?"

"Almost." With a flourish, Ash initiated a scan of the samples.

Tobin peered at the machine, watching it work on all of the samples. "How did you do that?"

"I told Traverse to process those soil samples. Soil science is an important branch of science, Tobin."

Olympia threw her hands in the air. "Have you ever noticed that you're terrible at prioritizing?"

"I'm a tactical genius. Just ask Simon," said Ash. "But this analysis is definitely the most important thing."

"Why?"

"Because the weapon-grade banquet probably isn't going to work."

"The what?" said both Olympia and Tobin.

Then, on Traverse's screen, the whole problem cracked wide open. Ash lost herself in a haze of numbers, logs, and biological analysis to the exclusion of everything else. The full display of Kett's curse lay before her. Three proteins each from three kinds of cells triggered nine dormant strands of DNA in sequence. It was the nine children from Kett's story. Ash blazed through the data with a fury she hadn't felt in years, coursing through pages and pages of data readouts. Kett's advanced case, Simon's moderate one, and hers—her case had just begun.

And it was incredible. She had already changed on a cellular level.

"This is terrifying," said Tobin.

There was more. Three proteins triggered the change, three proteins arrested it. Kett only carried the first three, so he kept changing. But could she...

"Only six," Ash said, disappointed.

"You were expecting more?" asked Tobin.

"Seven, actually."

He furrowed his brow.

"I got it!" she shouted.

Olympia jumped. "What?"

Tobin peered at the screen. "Oh, my." His voice sounded almost impressed, and Ash felt a little flutter of pride.

Ash looked around. The room was dark and heavy with silence. "How long has it been?"

Olympia stared at Ash. "It's the middle of the night, Ash, and I have a headache."

"Huh."

"Well?" Tobin said. "What did you find?"

"Oh!" Ash pushed her finding up to the big screens. "There's a cure."

"For what?"

"For everything. I've started printing a biopack with the three proteins. We can slot it into the emitter and distribute to everyone in town if we need to. It'll be perfect because this shouldn't do anything to anyone not affected by Kett's curse, but it'll cure anyone already in an advanced stage."

Olympia stared at Ash, blinking slowly. "Shouldn't? Did you say, *shouldn't*?"

Tobin peered at the screen. "This doesn't make sense."

It was Ash's turn to be smug. "Of course, it makes sense. There are three protein triggers that start a gene expression here." She jabbed at the screen. "Then three that make it stop here." She showed him a three-dimensional render of the chemicals involved. "It's as simple as that. One set starts it moving, one set stops it."

"But this cure of yours doesn't reverse anything," he said.

"I was exaggerating!"

The bioprinter door slid open, revealing a single,

compact biopack. Ash held it in front of Olympia. "This is a cure. It's the other half of the Seasider's curse. It arrests the changes happening in those affected, and by balancing the presence of those proteins, we'll be able to adapt humans for a life better suited for the planet and stop any bouts of uncontrollable rage."

"Listen to yourself, Ash. These proteins trigger something already coded into everyone's DNA? Simon's affected, so we must all have it. Who designed that? What is it for?"

A screen went black.

"Ash," Olympia said.

"It's designed by the architects," said Ash. "This is all part of the plan to adapt life to this planet. It went off the rails somewhere along the way, but right now this is a tool we can work with."

Another screen went black. Then another. Olympia said, "Traverse, sound the alarm."

"These are tools, Tobin. Nothing more. And right now we need to use these tools to solve something afflicting these people you're thinking of as enemies. If we cure them, or at least stop the changes, we can help them regain control."

Then all of the monitors went black, and Ash finally noticed.

The colony alarm sounded in a long wail loud enough to rattle Ash's teeth.

Ground shook under their feet. Dust and debris crashed through the door, washing over the scientists.

Ash tumbled to the floor. Olympia staggered back and hit the desk hard.

Ash yanked the tablet from its data harness and stuffed both it and the biopack in the biggest pockets of her coat. "Get her somewhere safe," she told Tobin.

Tobin grabbed Ash's arm as she moved to the door. He met her gaze with fierce determination. "What you've discovered is dangerous."

Ash pulled her arm away. "So, do I have committee approval to use this?"

He blinked. "I don't think you understand how committees work. Just be careful."

"Well, careful won't anyone any good. I need to be fast." Slapping a mask on her face to filter out smoke and dust, Ash ran into the oncoming disaster.

CHAPTER THIRTEEN

HOWLS ECHOED against the jet-black night. Somewhere deep in the distance, the attack had started,
and the double thump of the sonic cannons thun-
dered in the night. Ash crossed the square to the
Commons, circling the large building to find the
entrance she knew would take her where she needed
to go.

A group of colonists ran past her in their odd
monochrome clothing. They carried energy weapons
and ran with purpose. They would clash with the
enemy at the edge of town. People would be killed,
but if she could stop the attack with her cure, maybe
that death would be avoided. The emitter would
deliver the triggering protein to the whole colony and
everyone in it. She could stop this.

Only she could stop this.

A figure emerged from the hospital wing. Ludolf,
recognizable in his top hat, limped forward. He

carried a tension in his shoulders she hadn't seen before, as if the weight of the colony rested there.

He tipped his hat, and as he came closer, Ash saw the ragged state of his fancy clothing. "I'm sorry, Ash Morgan," he said, his accent thicker than ever.

Sorry for what? "You need to find somewhere safe."

A weak smile twisted the corner of his lips. "There's nowhere safe tonight, I'm afraid."

Behind him, a monstrous figure stepped out of the hospital.

Kett.

The giant man loomed over Ludolf, and for a long moment did nothing. His golden eyes danced from Ash to Ludolf, then to Ash again. What was he waiting for? Ash stood frozen in fear.

"She treated me well," growled Kett.

"Well, then," Ludolf said, "I suppose it would be best to keep this civilized, then."

Ludolf retreated upslope back toward the edge of town. He gestured for Kett to follow.

And he did.

Ash stood in the middle of the street, trying to grasp what she'd just seen. Ludolf and Kett working together.

She didn't have time to think about it before the pain hit. Ash doubled over at her waist. A wracking agony seized her lungs. Vision blurred. Her mouth tasted of coppery blood.

Far away, she heard explosions in the night,

higher and sharper than the sonic cannons. Smoke drifted through the square.

The red moon rose low over the mountains. Dusky red burned in the sky like the embers. Anger roiled through the smoke and dust. It caught in the back of her throat and clamped onto her chest like an iron bar. She clenched her fists and cast about in the haze.

Wind blew through the colony streets, blotting out the sky with thick smoke. The clamp released on Ash's chest. The anger ebbed. She stared at the wounds on her wrists. They burned like they were on fire.

She pulled the biopack from her pocket and stared at it. Kett's curse had her. She was already succumbing to their influence, just as Simon had. Those three cursed proteins burned through her system, and her only chance to avoid the anger of the red moon was to get that biopack to the emitter. Only that would stop the changes and halt the attack.

Kett was free. If he was out, then Simon might also be free.

Or dead.

Another explosion rocked the night, sending new waves of smoke and destruction through the skies. What was wrong with their defenses?

Find Simon or save everyone? Those were the choices. He could be lying wounded and dying from a savage attack from Kett, but if she didn't get to the emitter, people would die. More people. She had no doubt the fighting was already deadly. Simon wouldn't want that. Even if that were the only thing he could do to help, he would do it.

"Sorry, Simon," she whispered, surprised at the dry rasp of her voice.

Running to the Commons, she pushed her way through the door. The floor of the cantina swayed under her feet and the walls stood at a crooked angle. Ash stumbled as she felt her way through the smoke-filled halls.

Orson appeared through the haze, holding his side. The left side of his pastel-blue robes clung to his body in a dark, sticky mess. Blood.

Ash rushed to his side. "Orson, you have to get out of here."

Even as she said it, the building shuddered under the force of another faraway explosion. The city cracked under this pressure, and here in the center, the faults were worst of all.

Orson collapsed into a chair. "They came through the side door."

"You'll be fine," Ash said. She took his hand from where he held the wound. Dark blood oozed from the wound. She salivated at the smell of it, and the reaction triggered a wave of self-revulsion. "Orson, we need to get you over to the hospital wing."

Only, she couldn't. She needed to go straight to the emitter. The abstract idea of Simon being in trouble was one thing. This was Orson. Here. Dying. She couldn't leave him.

Orson drew a shallow breath. "They wanted the children. In the hospital wing. The med techs fought them off."

"Come on." Ash got an arm under his armpit and helped him up. She was sure every first-aid class she'd ever tuned out had said not to move injured people in this way. Every instinct of her biological studies told her that this might make things worse—tearing apart tissue that might not be otherwise damaged. But he had to move, and he was far too big for her to move on her own.

Orson stumbled, and she caught him. Outside, someone howled, and others joined in. The call was a half-animal, half-human sound, like a human doing their best imitation of bestiality. Or, possibly, the most horrible beast doing its best imitation of humanity.

She pushed through a stuck door, battering it open into the entryway to the hospital wing. The red-haired med tech rushed past the end of the long hall, ducking from room to room. He didn't take notice of Ash and Orson, and it was so far. So very far. Ash heaved Orson forward, and with every step, he helped less and less.

Halfway down the hall, he stumbled, but she hefted him up again. After several more steps, he fell again, and this time she couldn't get him up. The best she could manage was to ease his descent.

"Orson," she said. "We have to get you up. You have to keep moving." To the tech at the end of the hall, she called, "Help!" but he was far too busy with his own problems. Injured colonists poured in from fighting on the streets.

"Ash," whispered Orson. "It's okay."

She shook her head no. "We're almost there."

He took her bloody hands in his. Why was there so much blood? The wound in his side—the signature four scratches, same as Ash had on her wrist—pulsed with fresh blood. He pulled her hand close to his chest and said, "You were always my favorite, Ash. Out of all of them."

"Of course," said Ash, instinct driving her words even though she understood the absurdity of her ego. "I'm just great."

"If only you would learn to slow down," Orson said. "If only..."

He didn't speak for a long time, while shouts rang down the long hall. Ash thought that maybe someone had noticed them there, that they might come rescue Orson with all the tech and skill that the colony of Edge had to offer.

But it wouldn't be enough. When she forced herself to look right at the wound without shrouding herself in denial, she saw that the wound was worse than she'd initially thought. The cuts went straight through flesh and cut viscera. Her friend. Her good friend and the best drink mixer she'd ever known.

How absurd was that?

It was as absurd as her denying his injury. Denying the truth. "You'll be fine, Orson. Fine. Look, we can get through this. Your cantina is going to get a remodel from this. A big one. You can have that fancier bar you always wanted, and you can mix new kinds of drinks. Maybe I'll even use my biolab to grow you some new flavors. You'd like that, wouldn't you? Or do you get enough from Juliette?"

Orson listened to her ramble without interrupting. When she'd finally worn herself out, he squeezed her hand and said, "That's what I'm saying, dear. You're just too smart to hear it. Slow down." His throat clicked when he swallowed. "Slow down and think things through."

The ground shook. The hazard suits hanging in the nearby open closet swayed from the vibrations.

"No," Orson said as if he knew her intention. "It's too late. You have too much to do to worry about an old man like me."

With that, Orson breathed one last breath and closed his eyes. His kindly old face went slack.

He left this world forever, and Ash felt only the red-hot anger of grief burning deep in her chest.

CHAPTER FOURTEEN

Ash stood beneath the clear dome at the top of the Commons building. The protective glass shone in the moonlit night, and Ash again had a clear view of the dusky red third moon. The angry moon. Yaz, as Kett called it. She drew the biopack from her pocket and peered once again at its label. This was the tightly packed material that she needed to save the colony. Three simple proteins packed in such a way that they would feed into the emitter to disburse through the entire town of Edge.

The emitter itself sat like the twisted remains of a strange beast. It combined Pyramid technology, with tentacles and slick, black metal and Edge tech with its sleek lines and rigid angles. The device stretched high up under the dome, a braided array stretching out to join a tower that soared high above the colony. Below, a square chamber sat between two tables cluttered with mechanical debris.

She looked through the dome down at her beloved colony. Down at the end of a long street, a group of four monsters fought against a defensive cluster of colonists. Far away, she saw movement near Hector's arch.

Waves of smoke roiled low across the streets, slipping between tall buildings and enveloping the short ones. Thick, black clouds poured from waypoints at the corners of each new settlement. Many street corners held red-hot embers where once there had been defensive turrets. The defense grid had been activated when the alarm sounded—and everything else had failed.

Catastrophically.

The town was truly defenseless.

Ash pulled the lever to open the emitter chamber.

The old biopack that came out was far larger than the one she'd brought with her proteins. It smelled of burnt oranges and overheated granite, but when she pulled it free it fell to the floor in a solid thump.

"Stupid," she muttered to herself. She had assumed that the biopack the emitter used was the same size that Juliette had given her with the food samples. "Converter," she whispered to herself. The rasp of her voice made her glance at the moon again. It watched her like a bloodshot eye, but it didn't make her feel the insensible rage she had felt before. She drew a deep breath and dug through the supply cabinet.

Her biopack couldn't go in as it was. It would rattle around the chamber and cause a malfunction. She needed a converter or a way to brace it in the center of the chamber so that it didn't fall loose. Working furiously fast, she lashed the biopack onto a metal bracket that she pulled from the garbage bin.

Too big. It wouldn't fit through the opening. Ash swore.

Outside her chamber, down where the food science building grew like a fungus from the granite cliff, something burned so bright Ash had to look away.

Her comm unit crackled.

"Palak?" she said into the unit, remembering the army. "How soon can you get back?"

"We found it," said Palak through a haze of static, her voice echoing in the little chamber. "It's all ruins."

"They're here," said Ash as the ground shook once again. "We need you back."

"It's a fishing village, but it's all abandoned."

"I have a cure, but I don't know if it'll work." Ash swallowed hard. Her mouth was so dry. "It's untested." When Palak didn't answer, Ash said, "You have to come back. You won't find monsters there."

The only response was a burst of clicking static.

"It's only when they come out that they turn into monsters. I think there's a radiation trigger." Ash listened to her own words, then looked up at the red moon. Kett's story had said that Yaz had built a citadel on the red moon to watch over her people and deliver her curse. "A radiation trigger."

Her curse. A radiation trigger for the proteins. The final, seventh component of the transformation.

She looked down at the biopack in her hands. If she bent the bracket she could probably fit it in the chamber. She'd easily deliver the three protein triggers to the entire colony. She twisted the metal and crammed the whole thing into the emitter chamber. A safety lock clicked into place and the device started to hum.

"Ten minutes?" Ash exclaimed, staring at the readout. Too much time.

Orson had said to slow down. Slow down and think.

Outside, a colorist rammed a spear into a monstrous man's chest, only to have it break. He roared and colonists scattered.

"We found an entrance," said Palak through the comm, clear and strong. "We're going in."

"Wait," Ash said, fighting to balance her thoughts. "Can you hear me? You have to come back."

"We have this."

"No. Everything is failing. We're defenseless, and we need you back."

Palak swore. "You were supposed to have it under control."

"Well, I maybe don't." Ash bit her lip. "Get in there. Maybe we can still negotiate peace."

"Who negotiates peace with monsters?"

"I do," Ash said. "All the time."

The pieces of the puzzle were falling into place, and she thought she had some idea of what was really happening. Who was pulling the strings and how they were getting pulled.

"Traverse," she said, setting her tablet down on the workbench in front of her.

The AI's elaborate *T* logo spun silently for several seconds before the screen opened up for her commands. She scanned the log to see if her words triggered any warnings.

"Bring up a model of the three protein triggers that the Seasiders already have."

Traverse showed the modeling in several different ways, from the movement at a molecular level to the effects on the body. She watched as the neutral human form changed slowly to gain many of the features she only saw on the Skylings. Actual transformation of adult humans into a form that could better survive this planet: stronger bones, variably functioning lungs, filtered breathing, claws. She'd never quite understood the claws or sharp teeth, but now it almost made sense. She watched as glands formed at the base of each claw and the salivary glands mutated.

In the emitter chamber, her sample glowed a dull orange.

"Their modified bodies produce the three

proteins." Unsurprising, but pretty cool. "Extremely cool."

The changes to the brain were subtler. Adjustments in the endocrine system led to a powerful adrenaline response. Changes in eyesight corresponded with certain areas gaining an emphasis—and others getting starved. Ash didn't know human brains well enough to know for sure, but the areas that governed impulse regulation and hunger looked to be the most widely modified. She shuddered at the thought of that same change happening in her own brain. It explained the odd reactions to smells and the terrible impulse control.

"I've always had fantastic impulse control," she said out loud to Traverse. "So, there."

No warnings in the logs. This information must be exactly what Traverse wanted her to see. Outside, another explosion rocked the night. Smoke engulfed her lookout, and for a time her only experiences of the world were the murderous screams in the night and the shattering thump of violence breaking her world. She had to hurry.

Slow down.

"Show me the effects of the three new proteins," Ash said. "The three associated with stopping the mutations."

Traverse modeled these three changes atop both the baseline human and the monstrously deformed human. Changes in the brain reverted. Changes to the body normalized, stabilizing the rapidly changing system to something that might survive better in the long term. This trigger, timed right, completed a change that would allow her and others like her to survive Sky's difficult environment. Over generations.

Like Kett's people.

Only, they didn't thrive, did they? If what Kett had said was true, they barely scrounged out their lives underground, from generation to generation, and only those blessed with the transformation were able to wander far from their settlement because—

Because.

The smoke parted and Ash peered up at the red moon through her radiation-proof glass.

The biopack was bright orange now, lighting the room in its warm glow. The emitter started to hum.

"Traverse," she said, "show me what happens if the radiation trigger from the red moon is present during the application of all six proteins."

Warnings flew across the cracked screen. Ash couldn't read what was written there, but she didn't need to. *This* was something Traverse didn't want her to know. This was the forbidden knowledge she wasn't supposed to have.

On the screen, there were three simulatons playing out in various levels of detail. The baseline humans had no reaction to the red moon's radiation. Those exposed to only the first three proteins experienced extreme, rapid development in their endocrine reactions. Adrenaline pulsed through their systems.

Whole sections of their brains went dark and dormant. Skin hardened and their muscles gained superhuman strength.

Those exposed to the last three proteins, however, died. Their brains went dark fast, and Ash considered this a mercy because what happened next would probably haunt her dreams. Flesh fell from their bones, as the proteins wreaked havoc through shattered DNA. Cartilage melted and eyes bled. Bones grew weak and shattered.

Ash stared in horror at the biopack in the emitter.

It would be the death of them all.

Slow down.

Ash smashed the safety release and ejected the biopack. It fell on the floor with a thump, smoking where her makeshift frame had come in contact with the emitter chamber walls.

She didn't move for a whole minute, while the world of chaos swirled around outside the dome. Predators ran through the street, tracking their prey by smell or with haunting golden eyes. The angry red moon rose higher in the sky, unhindered by the billowing black of smoke and ash. The attack was in full swing, with the Seasiders raging through town in packs and the colonists fleeing.

But why?

Why attack? She didn't see the mindless consumption of the Anvil attack. Nowhere did the monsters stop and feed mindlessly upon the fallen. In fact, the way they moved didn't seem mindless at all.

They moved through town in ways that caused the most chaos.

There were plenty of fallen they could have taken. People she loved. People she knew. Strangers. The tight fury of grief clenched like a fist in Ash's chest. Panic gripped her, and she drew her breath in quick gasps. All that tragedy. All that anger. Outside of her dome, her world decayed into chaos, maybe never to recover.

Every defense had failed, of course. Every design involving Traverse's guidance had been flawed. Energy weapons exploded in their wielder's hands. Spears broke from weak materials. Traps and energy cannons failed outright or misfired, hurting the colonists. Orson was dead. Orson, who spent all his time in the very center of the city, was dead by a monster's claw. Kett's claw.

Edge was truly lost.

But why?

Ash turned her focus, scanning a city that was still very strange to her. Then, she found it. Olympia and Simon's house at the edge of town.

The children. Ludolf had been obsessed with the children. His people had failed to take the newborns from the hospital. Where would they go next?

She thought back to that first night back in Edge when she met Ludolf. He had seen Olympia's children and been struck by their strangeness. Ash had thought the reaction from him was his prejudice as an Anvilite fresh from the ship, but if he were a spy from the Seaside, he would not have known that the mutation could be stable. His people always suffered when the red moon rose. They knew the curse of their strangeness. If they had access to the Skylings, they might raise a generation of their people whose mutations were stable. They could finally thrive.

Slow down.

Ash drew a long, slow breath, considering her options. There were kids in danger. It was time to act, but first, she had to *think*.

Her hand fell on a lump in one pocket, and a grin spread across her face. No, it was time to *act*.

CHAPTER FIFTEEN

THE PROTECTIVE SUIT was too big in some places and too tight in others, but its powered limbs and sleek black style thrilled Ash to no end. She stepped from the Commons with her reinforced coat draped over the back of her fully enclosed suit, and the clear armored helmet glinted in the red moonlight.

With the suit blocking the radiation trigger, she didn't feel the effects of the angry moon. She tested the power suit with a loping jog upslope, amazed at how quickly it moved her from one street to the next.

Then, she jumped. Leaping high up above the short buildings, she could see all the way to Olympia's house. It glowed a furious orange and smoke billowed from its depths. Fire. Something inside was burning, putting everyone in danger. The children, Olympia. Everyone. Her thoughts went to Simon, who couldn't be there to help his family because of her.

She ran, but a Seasider in a pea coat leaped at her from an alley. Claws raked across Ash's coat and dragged her to a stop. Ash shoved hard, and the monster tumbled across the pavement, her bowler cap flying from her head.

"Sorry!" Ash shouted as she dashed away. In truth, she wasn't *all that* sorry, but it always paid to be polite.

As she approached Olympia's house, she slowed to a walk. Smoke billowed from the windows, and an orange glow made phantoms against the haze-filled night. The house itself wasn't flammable, but much of what made a house comfortable inside would certainly burn. She checked the suit's clock. Too soon.

Olympia sat against the wall in the shadows across the street. Ash approached, but the woman waved her back, coughing.

In a ragged voice, Olympia said, "They're still inside."

Inside.

An explosion shook the ground under Ash's feet. Deeper in the city, a new plume of smoke rose against the towering black buildings. She pulled her coat close, hoping that she added fireproof to the properties of her hastily generated clothing.

"Hide," Ash said to Olympia, not bothering to wait around for the woman to not comply. "I'll go in."

Ash forgot the strength of her protective suit and kicked the door clean off its hinges. A wave of heat burst from the house. She couldn't smell the smoke, but it blinded her. She fumbled with the suit's visual enhancements and found something that showed her shadows dancing in the smoke. It displayed the forms of larger objects and maybe—just maybe—the movement of anyone inside.

A sofa across the room burned furiously, so Ash passed that room and went down the hall. Where had the children been?

Upstairs. She pushed past a collapsed barricade. There had been fighting here. She read the frantic battle in the destruction apparent under waves of black smoke. Claw marks gouged huge tracks in the walls and Ash flashed back to the torn hole in Orson's side. She battered the remains of the barrier aside and mounted the steps several at a time.

Punching through another broken door, she burst into the children's room.

Kett looked up at her from where he crouched near the open window. Ash caught a shadow of movement outside on the roof.

All of Ash's kickboxing practice went straight out the door when several hundred pounds of vicious, frothing monster hit her hard in the chest. Claws slashed. Teeth snapped.

She shoved him back, but even with her powered suit, she could do little. Teeth sunk into her shoulder, sending daggers of pain as his jaw crushed the muscle.

But the teeth didn't penetrate her coat. He didn't draw blood.

Ash took hold of Kett's wrist with one hand and twisted. His grip fell loose, and he yowled in pain.

"I don't want to hurt you, Kett."

Kett snarled. Bit.

She snatched his other wrist. Holding both, she danced backward every time he tried to bite. The pain in her shoulder burned every time they moved. She'd have to finish this quickly if she wanted to finish it at all. She'd have to kill him.

Slow down.

The children weren't there. Nobody but Kett. Ash took in the rest of their surroundings. Something about the floor didn't look right in one corner. Kett slammed her into the wall.

Kett was injured. Badly. Blood soaked his chest and legs from a wound in his collarbone. She twisted and pushed, angling her pressure. He buckled and yowled.

"Let me help you " Ash shouted.

But outside the window, she could see the red moon. It still triggered Kett's mutations. Still whipped him into useless fury. She couldn't let him go or he'd attack again.

Ash dropped her weight, twisted hard, and threw Kett toward the corner. The floor collapsed like it was made of paper, and he fell.

Smoke and cinders burst from below, and Kett screamed. Her enhanced vision wavered. His cries were piteous, horrible things. He wasn't dead. He had killed Orson, but did she really want him dead?

The window stood open, and outside was a rooftop of another section of the house. Ludolf must have escaped that way with the children. She could leave, abandoning Kett to his fate. Ash took a step toward the window, which was barely visible through the boiling black smoke.

Then, she heard Kett's, "Please," spoken in a plain voice from somewhere close in the room.

Ash tasted smoke, thick and dry. Either the smoke overwhelmed her filters or Kett had managed to puncture her suit. Whatever the cause, she couldn't stay long. She plunged back into the worst of it, feeling along the floor until she located Kett's arm. His claws dug into the fibrous flooring, and his feet dangled over the fire below. Ash grabbed his wrists and, without bothering to wait for his cooperation, pulled as hard as she could. The big man launched from the hole and flew over her head, crashing into the wall next to the window.

"Sorry!" she shouted, and this time she was genuinely *almost* sorry, but Kett was kind of a jerk, so maybe not really at all.

Kett groaned.

She scooped him up under his armpits, aware that it must hurt like hell with his wound. She had little choice. Even with the strength the suit lent her, he was so much bigger she didn't have many options for moving him. She dragged him out the window onto the flat roof, and he collapsed into a bloody heap.

Ash checked her clock. Soon. Seconds, even, if she calculated it right. She felt the bone-deep ache of anger welling up in her and checked the integrity of her suit. A single tear ran along her shoulder where a claw had cut through her coat. She swallowed back the churning in her belly and gripped Kett hard.

"Where are the kids?" she shouted.

Kett growled through bloody teeth, "You're monsters. All of you."

Monsters? Ash let the man drop and stepped away. He collapsed and lay facing the sky. Rage still bubbled under the surface of his flesh.

Far away, another explosion rocked the night. Kett said, "Your people murdered mine. You've raised the promised children as your own. Ludolf is right. You worship your god and do only its vicious bidding."

"And you're obsessed with doing Ludolf's bidding. That guy is obsessed with being civilized."

"He wants only for our children to be free."

Ash pointed up at the red moon. "What about Yaz? Are they your god or a normal person? When they tell you to rage, you tear each other apart! You attacked *our* colony, Kett. You're stealing *our* children."

He shook his head. "We came in peace. When your people saw us they attacked. We had no chance at all. There was nowhere for our people to find safety from the angry moon."

She believed him. The anguish he and his people must have endured must have been terrible, and now they find a colony that isn't suffering at all—one that appears to be taking the children they were promised and raising them as their own. Ash wasn't sure if she could ever forgive Kett for killing Orson, but she didn't want him dead.

"We're not monsters," Ash said. "And neither are you."

Ash's comm unit crackled to life. The sound made her heart jump up to her throat.

Palak's voice said, "We're in control of Seaside."

"What?" Ash replied.

"They left their elderly people and their children here. Undefended. It's strange, Ash. They're all wearing suits and they bow to each other every time they meet."

"They're obsessed with the trappings of civilization," Ash said as the realization came to her. "It's how they compensate for a curse that makes them savage."

Palak said, "Yeah, well it's creepy. They haven't spotted us, though. We'll move in soon."

"I'd rather you come back this way. The town is currently under attack."

Palak didn't respond. Ash's comm unit wouldn't say whether or not the message got through.

Ash checked her clock one last time. Seconds.

"You see," said Kett. "Who is the monster now?"

"Probably Traverse for selectively censoring my conversations."

Kett glared at her.

Atop the Commons building, high above the glass dome, the emitter chamber lit up like a beacon in the night. It shone its warm yellow glow across all of Edge, touching the gate Hector had built all the way to Ash's tiny house on the outskirts of town. It hummed in the night and cut through billowing clouds of smoke.

Kett tensed. "What have you done?" He wrenched himself to his feet. "I have to stop you. This is the future of my people. The children will help us finally remove the curse."

All over town, fighting ceased and members of all the colonies turned toward the glowing orb that was the Edge emitter. Ash had no doubt the designs for the device came from Traverse. It was a delivery mechanism that would affect the entire town in a single flash. She had almost loaded poison into that chamber. It would have killed everyone in seconds.

"I'm sorry about this, Kett," she said. This time she meant it.

The emitter let out a low buzz and the air filled with a suffusion of particles.

Kett's expression changed from anger to curiosity to abject horror. He shouted and grasped at his own face as if he might somehow pull away the horrid scent of Spice Number Six, Juliette's greatest weaponized food-science creation and possible war crime.

"Where are they?" Ash asked Kett as he dropped to his knees. "Where are the children?"

From atop the roof of Olympia and Simon's house, she scanned the streets. Everywhere, clusters of Seasiders broke off from the stragglers of colonists. Seasiders staggered and retched, affected by the emitter's horrid scent.

It wasn't an instant banquet, but Ash supposed it would work as the next best thing. Disabled by the assault, the Seasiders couldn't properly fight. They broke away and fled in pieces.

But somewhere, Ludolf still had several of the Skyling children, including Olympia's triplets. Spice Number Six would force them to flee, but that meant Ash had less time to stop them.

She knew exactly where they were going and where they would need to pass in order to leave the colony.

Ash ran.

CHAPTER SIXTEEN

THE ARCH WAS a thing of beauty up close: formed of black stone and carved in intricate detail. Hector hadn't built a wall to keep people out or a gate that could be locked against invaders. Hector had built a gigantic greeting for visitors, and he'd poured every ounce of his soul and artistry into it.

"I love that guy," she said. Her breath still came in deep gulps from the run. Even with the mechanical assist of the powered protective suit, reaching the arch before the retreating Seasiders had been difficult.

Ludolf led the group. Under his fancy hat, his eyes watered, and his nose ran. Spice Number Six from the emitter wasn't quite so strong this far from the Commons, but it still affected them.

The other Seasiders with him suffered similarly. These were the monsters she had seen around town. They wore ragged suits like Ludolf, and several wore long, frayed dresses, all in muted, mixed tones rather than the color-coded clothing Traverse had been printing recently. Many of them were noticeably transformed, with ridges of mutated flesh and wicked claws. They looked tired and furious all at once as if the night's activity had worn them in ways Ash could not imagine.

With them came the Skyling children, ranging in age from infants to school-age miscreants.

"Skye, where are you going?" She asked the boy as he came leading two of the smaller Skylings.

He looked at her and bared his teeth in what she hoped was a smile. "You didn't come visit," he said.

"I was busy!" She took a step forward. "You can't leave with them, Skye."

The boy put a protective arm around the shoulder of the younger Skyling. "These people can help us."

Ash stood in the center of the gateway with fists on her hips. "So, that's why you're here, Ludolf? To take our children?"

Ludolf's face was a twisted snarl. "You have no claim to these children."

Casting a glance at Skye, Ash said, "They're not exactly old enough to make their own decisions." When Skye opened his mouth to protest, she cut him off, "You're not, Skye. You have people here who love you." The pain of guilt in her chest grew wickedly sharp. "I'm sorry I didn't come visit you right away."

When Skye frowned his young age became more

apparent. He'd been a toddler only a couple years ago, and he might grow fast, but he wasn't old enough to be on his own. Still, he had that stubborn streak. Instead of backing down, he ushered his wards closer to the pack of Seasiders. "They won't leave us."

Ludolf tugged at the cuffs of his suit coat. "You're not going to stop us, Ash. Please don't try."

"You feel it, don't you?" Ash flipped a switch and removed her helmet. A rush of adrenaline rolled over her, but she swallowed it back. She needed to speak face to face with Ludolf if she wanted to stop this for good. "The anger, the power. It's all triggered by radiation from the red moon. From Yaz."

His fists clenched so tight his knuckles went white.

Ash said, "But you control it somehow. You build the whole structure of your civilization around self-control. You aren't monsters. You're using the blessing to do exactly what you've decided to do."

Ludolf tugged at the frayed corners of his suit. "The hallmark of civilization is to resist our savage nature."

"You're stealing our children."

"*Our* children," Ludolf snarled. Then, he smoothed the crisp lines of his suite. Ash saw clearly now that the suit was old. Ancient, really. Its pockets were frayed and the elbows worn thin. "You don't know how much they mean to us. They'll free our people."

"*Science* will free you," Ash said. Her heart

slammed in her chest, and adrenaline made her hands jittery.

The Seasiders circled, pulling the children with them to form an oval around Ludolf and Ash. Their hollow eyes tracked her every move, and their silence lay like heavy fog under the towering arch. Even the children watched with quiet wonder. Skye stood with the others, watching her with his yellow eyes.

Ludolf removed his top hat and threw it to one of his people. "Your message of peace has drowned in bloodshed." His coat fell to the ground.

The comm unit clipped to Ash's shoulder crackled once. Then went silent.

Ash's brow furrowed. She couldn't tell if it was the trigger of the red moon or her own genuine anger bubbling in the back of her chest. "Your people attacked Anvil. You killed us. Tore them apart."

"We were starved from our homes, plagued by your reckless influence on the world. We set out to discover who would do such a thing. Who would so carelessly ruin our history and our lands? When we arrived we discovered that Yaz's influence is greater up here on the mountain, but you were *deserving* of their anger."

Ludolf lunged. Ash caught the glint of an obsidian knife in his hand mere seconds before it slashed at her throat. She dodged back, but the suit's power assist threw her off balance and she collapsed. Ludolf pounced on her, but she batted him away with a powerful backhand.

He landed with a sickening thud and a gasp of pain.

"You slaughtered our people," Ash said, dropping into her best kickboxing stance. Her style of kickboxing was more aerobic exercise than martial art, but she hoped a show might convince him not to attack. "You *ate* people."

Ludolf wiped blood from his lip. "Then slay us like the monsters we are."

More Seasiders arrived from town, filling in the oval around the two of them. Their powerful, muscular forms became the wall that Hector never built. Ash tried to ignore how they boxed her in. This was a discussion with Ludolf, and she had to concentrate on him or she had already lost.

Only, it was hard to concentrate. The fuzzy red anger washed through her bones.

"What's your plan, Ludolf?" she said. "Take our Skyling kids and hope you can fend off their furious parents?"

"These children are what we should have always been," snarled Ludolf. "And you'll let them live with us because they *are* us. Look at them! They possess the blessing without the curse. How can you possibly teach them how to live?"

Ash looked around at the bloody claws of the men and women surrounding her. The crowd seethed with barely controlled fury. "You think you represent a good example of how to control that power, but you let yourselves be ruled by fear."

"Only when you killed us!" Ludolf lunged, but this time Ash was ready. She snapped a kick out as he approached. It didn't land on his head as planned but hit his collarbone hard and spun him out and away.

He closed the distance again and slammed into Ash. Something cracked under her as she landed, and when she tried to roll away, her protective suit failed. It was dead weight.

She felt a familiar thump through the stony earth, like the heartbeat of a giant.

Ludolf smiled through his crooked teeth. "What's so great about what you would teach the children? How to ruin the planet? How to turn the sky brown with sludge and the seas black with death? Will you teach these children to be wonderful and perfect like yourself?"

The thumping grew louder. She could hear it now, in addition to feeling in the stone.

"We're not perfect." Ash pulled the cord in the front of her suit and sat up out of it as it fell away. She stood in front of Ludolf, and the wind whipped through her thin dark-blue scrubs. No power-assisted suit. No armored jacket. She raised her two small fists and looked Ludolf right in the eye. "We'll teach them that they will always be loved. That they will never be alone in this world, and that they can be whoever they need to be. We'll teach them that science can solve anything."

Ludolf met her gaze. "There are some problems science *shouldn't* solve."

Behind Ash, Hector's spider lumbered over the rise. Ash stood in the center of a crowd of Seasiders, her fists raised in defiance against a small army. At a wave of her hand, Hector stopped, his huge spider looming over the crowd.

"The children do not belong with you," Ludolf growled. "They need real structure. Civilization."

Ash lowered her fists. "They belong with their parents, and anyone who denies that can't very well call themselves civilized." One call to Palak and she could turn this into a hostage exchange. Everyone might walk away with their lives intact and their children at home—or they might not. Either way, it would be the start of enmity between the two civilizations that would likely last generations. "I know this place is a mess. Edge is unrecognizable, even though I was only gone a year. But there's still good here." She turned and met Skye's piercing gaze. "These kids belong here in Edge where they are already accepted and where people already love them. They aren't monsters, and neither are you." She looked at the Seasiders in the crowd. A group of Edgers approached from the colony carrying broken spears. If they closed the distance, there would be more violence. Ash thought of Orson and how he'd died protecting what he loved. "We have to slow down, Ludolf. All of us."

Ludolf snarled, 'We've seen how you treat outsiders."

Ash spread her arms wide, revealing the scratches

healing on her wrist. "I know you all feel it, but the moon's anger doesn't make you monsters. I feel it too. I've always felt it, even before your curse. But you can control it. You're better than this anger that's killing you. Better than the monsters that you might become."

But something changed behind Ludolf's eyes. His features twisted into rage. Sweat beaded on his forehead.

Hector's spider took a step forward through a parting crowd. With a click and a whoosh, its cutting torch flared to life.

Ash waved him back. "Ludolf, we've wronged you. Your people suffered under the changes we made to Sky. You came to Anvil and were seen as monsters. I get that. You came to Edge and saw that the only way forward for your people was a strike to distract us and to grab the children that Yaz promised your people. I agree with you. The children promise a better future." She took a step to the side, keeping herself between Ludolf and the spider. "Their DNA contains the keys to stabilizing your condition without killing you. We can be allies in this. Even friends."

Ludolf shuddered with rage, but he didn't attack. His face twisted. Turned red. "We can't trust her," he said to the Seasiders. "I've watched her lie. I've seen her steal."

Ash opened her mouth to protest, but before she could, her comm crackled to life.

"Seaside is ours, Ash," said Palak. "We've got your hostages."

Ludolf blinked. "You see?" he said. "Already she betrays us."

A discontent rumble rolled through the crowd.

"No, wait," Ash said.

Ludolf attacked. Claws raked at her shoulder and arm. Teeth snapped by her ear.

"No!" shouted Skye.

Hector's cutting torch swung in a wide arc. Down and across.

Ash grabbed Ludolf and pulled. The torch swiped empty air, the heat burning across them both. Ludolf slammed to the ground and continued his assault.

His teeth sunk deep into her hand, and Ash screamed in pain. Muscle tore and she tasted the pain in the back of her throat. Rage boiled up in her. Strength pulsed through her body, but it wasn't enough.

Light above her shifted. She grit her teeth against the pain, pulled her shoulder free, and once again pulled Ludolf to the side. With her own sheer strength, she yanked him out of the path of the cutting torch a second time. He flew several feet and slammed against a rock.

Ash bled on the ground. The spider's torch pulled back for another swing. Now that Ash and Ludolf were separated, Hector could strike the man down.

But the big man hesitated.

Ludolf did not. He rolled to his feet, braced himself, and pounced.

A streak of dark blue burst through the crowd and struck Ludolf hard in the side. A flash of teeth and claws lashed out at the blue form. Blood flew. Screams echoed against the arch and called out to the red moon above.

Then, everything stopped.

Simon stood from Ludolf's still form. His yellow eyes focused on Ash. He drew quick, ragged gasps of air. Somehow the archivist managed to ask the stupidest question he could possibly have managed. "Are you hurt?"

She gave the stupidest answer. "I'm fine." Despite the bold and obvious lie, she let Simon help her to her feet. She addressed the crowd. "This is enough," she said. To Palak, she said, "Let them all go."

Skye stared at her.

Ash spoke so all the Seasiders could hear. "You attacked because we threatened your settlement. We're sorry. It isn't what we meant to do."

A Seasider stepped forward from the crowd. His long gray hair fell over a nasty burn on half his naked chest. "Did you mean what you said?" he growled. "About us being welcome."

Ash beckoned him to walk with her through the gate so that they could look at it from the outside. "Can you read what it says up there just under the quadruple-life-size statue of a girl reading a book with her handsome boyfriend holding an umbrella over her?" she said, pointing at the uppermost reach of the arch. It was a nice statue.

"The script is foreign to me."

"Makes sense. Pyramid has its own script too. It says *All Are Welcome*, and if we're going to survive on Sky, then that's the philosophy we follow. You, your people, your families. They're always going to be welcome here." She looked the man straight in the eyes. "But you can't take our children."

The man glanced at Ludolf, who still lay bleeding on the ground. "And him?"

Ash flexed her hand where his teeth had torn through the flesh. It hurt so bad and she just wanted to cry. "I think he owes us a really serious apology."

CHAPTER SEVENTEEN

"Is this thing going to work?" Hector asked as he sat next to Ash on the bench. Their view overlooked a massive construction project of black metal and red glass. He'd been building it, but it was finally his turn for a break. Others from his construction crew fitted detailed pieces in place.

"Destroying the radiation source on Yaz will stop it from triggering the mutations that make people go crazy."

He closed his big warm hand over hers. "But will the laser be able to hit the source?"

Ash shrugged. "I'm not an astrophysicist."

"Yeah. Nobody is." Hector wiped the sweat from his forehead. "Traverse doesn't want us looking at the sky too much."

"The science behind this sky laser is good, and it doesn't use any fancy computing for targeting. We handcrafted every piece so it won't have any built-in flaws. We're able to locate the source of radiation on the surface of Yaz without Traverse at all, and lasers tend to fly pretty straight. It'll work."

"But will it blow up when we switch it on, like most of our defense grid?"

Ash shuddered at the tragic loss of life the colony had suffered when it tried to activate the Traverse-built defenses for the first time. She thought of Orson and drew a shaky breath. "I'm eighty percent positive that it won't."

"The engineers said ninety-nine percent," Hector said, but he took a step back, anyway.

Juliette sat on the other side of her on the bench and said, "You need to watch out for engineers."

Ash turned to her and smiled. The woman smelled of roses and freshly baked bread. "Yeah, engineers are the worst. Scientist fist bump." The two women knocked knuckles.

Hector said, "Can this be used for—you know—that other thing?"

Ash thumbed the paper notebook in her lap. The other thing. "We took a vote and decided that firing a really powerful laser at something covered in mirrors isn't the best way forward." Their ability to hit Traverse wasn't even guaranteed, since it didn't emit radiation like the station on Yaz. They could see the massive station as it passed in the night sky, but hitting it was another question.

"Shouldn't we be worried about destroying something important?" Hector asked. "Records or history or something."

The thought hadn't occurred to Ash. "It's probably fine."

Hector took a bite of his sandwich, which smelled something awful to Ash's odd senses. Without further exposure to Yaz's radiation, she had been able to arrest the changes in herself and others, but the changes she'd already experienced in her body were going to stay with her, including a tweaked sense of smell. Reversing them was too dangerous.

"Bergamot," Juliette said.

"What?"

"Spice Number Six? The one you vaporized in the emitter. It was a scent called bergamot. Very unique."

"It smells like tea," Ash said.

Juliette flashed a crooked smile. "A lot of people like it."

"Seasiders won't," Ash said, failing to keep the threatening growl from her voice.

"Ash," said Hector.

Juliette said, "Then they're welcome to avoid it."

Hector placed a hand on Ash's shoulder. "You have that meeting pretty soon."

Ash drew a long breath. The Seasider curse hadn't been in her system enough to cause any visible changes, but sometimes she wondered if her short temper was because of that or the fact that she hadn't slept well for weeks She gripped her notebook and walked beside Hector through town.

They passed a playground where Simon and Allan watched over a whole gaggle of children. Skylings and earthlings played with a few of the newer Seasider children. They looked like baseline earthlings, but Traverse would only print ocean blue clothing for them.

"Hey, wolfman," Ash called out to her friend.

Simon showed some definite changes before it was reversed. He seemed taller to Ash, but she'd measured and he hadn't really changed. Heavier, for sure, though. His muscle was more toned, and the rash around his nose marked the start of a filtering organ much like Skye's.

"Hey, Ash," said Simon. He crossed the playground to them and laughed as his children orbited him. "How are you healing?"

"Terribly." She eyed him. "You?"

He held up a bandaged hand. When Kett and Ludolf left him in the jailhouse he had broken his own thumb to get free. "This is the only thing that's not healing very fast."

"That's hardcore, Simon. Thanks for helping me."

He scooped Skye up with his good hand. "It seemed like the right thing to do at the time."

Ash watched awhile as he tossed Skye high into

the air several times. Skye would land with a cat's grace, crouching and peering at the other children around him. Then he would rush back for another go. Earthlings, Skylings, and Seasiders all pounced on Simon, and the whole lot fell over giggling.

"They know how to get along," Hector said.

"Yeah. It's easier for them." As they walked away, Skye broke from the group and ran over to them.

"You left me," he growled. "A long time ago."

"I'm sorry, Skye." She hadn't known it had even bothered him. Every excuse she could think of tasted like dust on the tip of her tongue.

"They said you would come back, but they didn't say when."

"We didn't know."

"I know," he mumbled.

Ash pulled the boy into a hug, and after a brief moment of tension, he melted into her as if he'd always belonged. She held him for a long time until she worried that the tears wetting her cheeks might drop onto his head. When she pulled away, she saw he had been crying as well.

"I won't leave you," she said, and she meant it. They stood in companionable silence for a while until Skye's nature caught up with him and he bolted off to play with other children his size.

It hadn't been easy for their new visitors to integrate. Tensions were still high on all sides, and Ash suspected they would be for quite some time. People had died in the conflict, and people struggled to understand what was really to blame. For Ash it was simple. She blamed herself.

Her blossom storms had devastated the Seasider community. Her insistence that the colonies not prepare for violence had led to Anvil being unable to halt an attack. She should have known that the weapons created with Traverse's help would break at the worst possible time. Traverse had never given them weapons before. Why start now?

Unless to lead them down this dangerous path.

Ash touched the panel on the outside of the Archives building. When it didn't respond, Hector tried. It opened without hesitation.

"That keeps happening to me," Ash said.

Hector took her hand and walked her in. "Traverse ignores most Seasiders entirely."

Moira met them at the elevator. Her white hair was pulled back in a formal braid. "They're ready for you down below." She punched a code into the elevator's panel.

Ash and Hector rode the elevator in silence. Dim light flickered as they plunged deeper and deeper below the rock. When the doors opened, Ash stepped forward, her footsteps hollow on the glossy marble floor.

Olympia sat at the head of the table, with the other scientists of the council in their usual places around the outside. Ludolf sat in an extra chair pulled up to one end and he shrank into it as she approached. The man wore a new top hat and suit, this time made of his people's ocean blue. The three other Seasiders at the table, including Kett, all wore the same color. They weren't scientists, but Ash supposed the council probably needed to start being a little more inclusive. Even Tobin accepted them at the meeting after only a little resistance.

Ash swallowed a sudden wave of stage fright, straightened her notebook, and started speaking. "Friends of the council, we've seen this day coming for a long time. From the day it tried to burn us with mirrors, and the day we learned it murdered our loved ones when they retired. Recently, we learned that it genetically engineered a kill switch into our DNA, so that it might one day eliminate us more easily. It has manipulated our love and our fears. It's dripped poison into our atmosphere for the pure scientific reason of discovering our reaction to it. For too long, Traverse has been our angry god above, distributing judgment at random and without mercy. It has been a scientist and we have been its unwitting subjects.

"I come with a message today, and that message comes with a plan. The plan has been worked over and over in my head for years, and it covers everything, from shoring up food systems to managing our atmospheric influences on the planetary scale. This plan requires nothing less than a significant risk to the survival of all colonies, and if you today vote not to take that risk, then I promise I will abandon it forever. I've taken my time to think this all the way through.

You risk death by following me, but I believe we guarantee obliteration by maintaining our current course. I have thought long and hard on this and come to one conclusion."

She slammed her notebook down on the table. "Traverse must be destroyed."

AUTHOR'S NOTE

As always, a special thanks goes out to my wife Carol and my boys Isaac and Gabe. Without their support none of this ever gets to happen.

Huge thanks also go out to my Beta Readers. Your insight is precious to me and helped make this a better book.

Writing a book may seem like a solo activity sometimes, but I'd never be here if not for support from the Rochester Writers Group, SFWA, and my fellow writers and readers over on my Patreon. The ability to surround myself with like minds keeps me sane and keeps the words flowing.

Thanks also go out to Scott Alexander Jones for fantastic editing that always seems to find ways to improve and amplify everything I write.

-Anthony W. Eichenlaub

www.ingramcontent.com/pod-product-compliance
Lightning Source LLC
Chambersburg PA
CBHW032145170626
46808CB00006B/2375